I0638385

VICIOUS

by ANDREA MURRAY

DMP

Dragon Moon Press

Copyright 2012 © Andrea Murray

This work is licensed under a Creative Commons Attribution-Noncommercial-No
Derivative Works 3.0 Unported License.

Attribution — You must attribute the work in the manner specified by the author or
licensor (but not in any way that suggests that they endorse you or your use of the work).

Noncommercial — You may not use this work for commercial purposes.

No Derivative Works — You may not alter, transform, or build upon this work.

**Inquiries about additional permissions
should be directed to: publisher@dragonmoonpress.com**

Cover Design by Greg Simanson

This is a work of fiction. Names, characters, places, brands, media, and incidents are
either the product of the author's imagination or are used fictitiously. Any resemblance
to similarly named places or to persons living or deceased is unintentional.

Print ISBN 978-1-988256-10-8
EPUB ISBN 978-1-988256-11-5

Library of Congress Control Number: 2014922649

This book is dedicated to every student who has ever asked,
"Mrs. Murray, can you help me pick out a book?"

PROLOGUE

THE FLAME OF A TALLOW CANDLE sputtered below the rim of the pewter candleholder, casting eerie shadows beyond the narrow circle of light it afforded. Shuffling in the darkness and shivering in her threadbare nightshift, the girl knelt and poked at the dying embers in the hearth. Outside, lightning momentarily lit the sky and the kitchen while thunder near rattled her already chattering teeth. Wind whistled around the edges of the door and whipped the branches of the budding oak tree outside the window.

"Curse this weather!" She grumbled to herself while she added a log to the fire then filled the heavy teakettle from a bucket near the fireplace. "Curse this hour!" Her grandmother used to say that during the witching time of night, evil women worked their magic, and ghouls sought the souls of the unborn. She unconsciously rubbed her rounded belly where her shift stretched tightly as she crouched in front of the crackling fire. Her babe, her firstborn, would arrive by the next full moon. She felt sure of it.

She prayed for a boy—a son, even an illegitimate one—would be valued, maybe even loved. If she had stayed in England she would be married by now. She should never have traveled to this godforsaken colony, but her father had given her no choice, indenturing her for four years to help reconcile his debts to a nobleman most considered insane, and when that nobleman packed his household for the colonies, she'd left her life, left England, and sailed to Jamestown. Grown now and nearing the end of her servitude, she wanted nothing more than to find some cottage and to live life for herself and her child.

Her fingers worried the ends of her long brown braid as she thought of her freedom. Mayhap Robert would leave with her. She knew his father, Lord St. Clair, would never agree to his only son marrying a servant little better than a slave, but Robert loved her. He would do right by her and the babe. She had to believe that. Robert didn't even know about their child since he'd left for England before she realized she carried, but when he returned, he'd set all to rights.

A boom of thunder made her gasp and jump; a shiver that had nothing to do with the chilly room raced along her spine and raised the hair on her arms. She rubbed the ache in her lower back that had troubled her all day and kept her awake. The sturdy ladder-back chair stood within reach, and she used it to push and pull herself awkwardly to her feet.

"Now, where did I put that cup?" She spoke aloud to the babe who kicked a reply as she lifted the candle to find the cup she'd already filled with the special tea blend the strange, old midwife had given her. Goody Smythe lived on the outskirts of Jamestown, nearly in the forest, and was feared by most of the respectable women in the settlement, but she was also the only midwife who would speak to an unmarried, indentured serving girl. Witch or no, for two months now, Goody Smythe's brew had eased her aches and somehow given her the energy she needed to stay on her feet and fulfill the grueling daily duties heaped upon her by Goody Crowe, the head of the household servants. Today, she had scoured the pewter dishes now gleaming in a hutch near the door to the servants' quarters.

Goody Crowe ruled the house servants with an iron fist in the absence of a proper mistress, Lord St. Clair having lost his wife two winters past. No excuses from work would be given to an unmarried servant girl with child, and she'd asked for none but rather counted herself lucky that she'd not been turned out when her growing child could no longer be concealed. Her master had been so busy with his work of late that she doubted he'd even noticed. He had never asked her about the child's father, but she would not have told him she carried his grandchild anyway. That was for Robert to do.

"There you are!" Picking up the cup in her other hand she turned back to the kettle that must surely be warm by now. Grabbing the towel from the scarred work table, she gingerly pulled the kettle hook toward her and lifted the heavy pot. She breathed in the pungent steam as she filled the cup to its rim then lifted it to her mouth. The familiar burn in her throat soon gave way to warmth that spread throughout her muscles and eased her aches.

Raising the cup in a mock toast, she said, "Thank you, Goody Smythe." She smiled and rubbed her swollen abdomen. "Robert will return, and all will be well, little one."

In answer, the clouds let loose a rumble. As a flash brighter than all the others drew her attention to the window, a searing pain ripped through her.

CHAPTER ONE

WHAT I NEED TO KNOW: Is my dad alive? How is he connected to the organization that kidnapped Aunt Charlotte? Where does this power come from?

What I know: My mother is dead. Aunt Charlotte is dead. My old life is dead.

Okay, not literally. As Aunt Charlotte used to say, pity party time, but I think that I deserve a few minutes of that even if I did choose this existence for myself. I lost everything when I chose to leave—my best friend Abby, my dream boyfriend Easton, and worst of all, my home with Aunt Charlotte.

I live, if you can call it that, in a closet-sized motel room turned apartment in what amounts to a truck stop where, as far as I can tell, the dot on the map is bigger than the town. When this town sprang up in the 1950s, it was an important stop on Route 66, the best way west. But it looks to have been dried up for longer than it was ever popular.

Besides the motel, there's a big gas station where trucks stopover for the night, a diner, and a mostly empty town square. Beyond the square, some depressed houses contemplate suicide while the July heat peals their paint. Overall, not super-inspiring.

In its prime, it probably looked like something from a black and white television show where moms baked cookies all day, kids learned valuable life lessons in half an hour, and dads... well they came home every night. I'd just like my dad to come home *one* night—that is if I still had a home. I would love to know my dad's name, see his face even if it's only a photograph. I lie awake every night, listen to the mice scurrying in the ceiling of this hole, and wonder if I look like him, sound like him. Did he love my mom? Did he leave us, or did we leave him?

I think about him, Aunt Charlotte, Abby, Easton, all missing from my life. At least I know staying away from Abby and Easton is probably saving their lives, something I couldn't do for Aunt Charlotte. I can almost hear her scolding me for blaming myself. "Vivian, sweetie, crazy psycho men with eyes like bottomless pits cannot be trusted," she would say, red curls spilling from beneath her gardening hat. It's only been three months since I lost her, but her face is already beginning to blur in my memory. If I were really a superhero like Easton accused me of being, I would have saved her from Hoyt Matthews and his henchmen.

Now, here I am, eating microwaved soup every day and trying not to brainjack the customers for tips in the diner where I waitress. I've been working my way west, Destination Unknown, USA, looking for something I can't even define. I just think I'll know when I get there (as if that makes sense even to me). I think I'll 'feel' that Mom was here or Dad worked there.

When I took off in Aunt Charlotte's car, I knew I'd never go back. I needed to become invisible to protect Abby and Easton and to keep Hoyt from finding me. The monsters have taken Aunt Charlotte, my mom, and most likely my dad. I won't let them have Abby or Easton, the two people on Earth unfortunate enough to care for me, and even though it's been hard, it feels good in a weird way to stand on my own, to only worry about getting from point 'A' to point 'B'. I haven't even been all that scared, just very, very lonely.

After leaving the park where all hell broke loose, I tossed my phone and stopped in the first big city out of state where I sort of mentally convinced—okay, forced—some poor city official to change my last name and driver's license to show my age as eighteen. I am now Vivian Vincent again, probably not smart returning to my childhood name, but that's quite likely not the stupidest decision I've made. I've answered phones, cooked greasy burgers, and handed out fliers dressed as a giant hot dog for a new franchise opening. Currently, I'm a waitress in a blue polyester uniform at a truck stop diner that reeks of fried onions and dirty feet. All of this so that I can work my way west to *wherever*, driving a car that I traded Aunt Charlotte's clunker in to get. Such a glamorous life!

Sounds like a great plan, huh?

CHAPTER TWO

GETTING UP THIS MORNING was torture after lying awake most of the night. The alarm sounded like a tornado siren, but a shower always makes me feel less comatose. Auburn hair pulled back, blue uniform zipped, tennis shoes on, I lock the door behind me and walk the half-mile to the diner where five semis are parked nearby.

"There's my star waitress!" Mr. Lewis's voice, gravelly from forty years of smoking, booms from behind the counter where two men sip coffee. "The sun is shining, and business is good!" He says that same thing every morning, rain, shine, customers or not. He's the happiest man I've ever met, and I think I'll actually miss him when I leave here. Of course, that might be a while since I'm making decent money despite the lack of life in this town. Mr. Lewis's diner does well since it is the only stop along this deserted stretch of highway.

"Morning, sir." I smile and nod to the two men at the counter. "I guess Julie's not here yet. Should I start filling the shakers?" I tie an apron with only a few stains around my waist.

"Julie's gonna be late, honey," he says, patting my back. "Think you can handle it awhile all alone?" He doesn't wait for my reply, already knowing my answer, and starts through the swinging door to the kitchen. "Alejandro is sick—least that's what he says—so I'll be manning the grill today. I think he doesn't want to sort through the supply shipment I got last night. He's sleepin' in the back room."

Connected to the diner is a small storage area where, between toilet paper rolls and stacks of industrial-size ketchup bottles, stands an old army cot. I slept there a couple of nights when I first arrived in town. I'd coasted in about 2:00 am on fumes and spent my last $2 on a bowl of chili and a glass of tea. Lucky for me, Mr. Lewis was working alone that morning. He offered me a slice of apple pie, and I burst into sobs. I guess he knew a stray when he saw one because he offered me the cot, then a temporary job. Julie's sister, Gwen, one of the other waitresses had started her maternity leave the day before I arrived, so my timing was perfect. That's the only thing about these last three months that has actually been easy.

When the morning sun begins to peek in the front windows, the truckers start to wander in for breakfast, and my shift officially begins with an order of ham and eggs from a big, bearded man. By noon, my feet ache. Customers have steadily streamed in all morning, and for a Thursday, we're really busy. Thankfully, I haven't had time to think about my family or feel sorry for myself, and I already have $30 in tips.

"Vivian, I'm so sorry!" Julie rushes past me, throwing her purse behind the counter and tying on her apron. "Joey got called in to work an extra shift, and I didn't have a sitter till Gwen got back from the doctor." She grabs an order pad and tucks it into her apron front. "He couldn't *not* go. We really need the money, and he makes double what I do, so… I'm late," she rambles while she looks for a pencil.

"That's okay, not a problem." I point to a table of three who need to place their order while I deliver a grilled cheese and fries to a man at the counter. Grabbing the pencil stub from behind my ear, I move on to a table near the side window where an old guy in an oil-stained cap is sitting.

"I want a steak, medium rare—not well done and not totally rare. But I better see blood when I cut into it, or you'll be getting it right back, girlie." He scowls at me while I smile sweetly. I really want to tell him where he can shove that medium rare, not well done, steak, but I need those tips even if it means being nice to grouchy, dirty jerks. "And sweet tea. You know what that means, girlie? Sweet, as in real sugar, none of that fake crap!"

"Is that all?" I'm scribbling the order and marking it 'rush' so that we can get this guy out of here quickly when I feel a tingle trip down my spine. The hairs on my arms stand up. I've felt that tingle before. Then it thrilled me; now it scares the hell out of me. I slowly lift my head to look out the window, knowing already what I'm going to see.

The sun glares off the windshield of an SUV, obscuring the faces within. The driver's door opens and strong fingers grasp the top of the door as he swings his long legs out. The tingle is so strong now it borders on painful. As the door closes, I see his face, aqua eyes clear even at this distance. Easton is walking toward the diner.

CHAPTER THREE

DANG! HE LOOKS GOOD in his khaki shorts and white t-shirt. His hair's a little longer, but it takes nothing from his beautiful face. Abby's voice pulls my eyes from him. She is bouncing along behind him, blonde curls pulled into pigtails and purple glasses perched on her perky nose, dragging a still super-size Cooper by the hand. She's smiling, probably jabbering about what she wants to eat. When she glances toward the window, I slam back to reality full force.

"Yes, uh, yes, sir. I'll be, uh, right back," I stammer, backing into the table behind me, shaking the drinks of the couple seated there. "Sorry, I'm so sorry!" I whirl away, ram my thigh into the corner of another table, and walk-jog my way to the kitchen. When the swinging door smacks my butt and knocks me farther into the room, I squeak, snagging Mr. Lewis's attention.

"Vivian, what's the matter? You're white as a sheet. You see a ghost?" Still holding his spatula like a shield in front of him, he comes toward me with real concern on his face and in his voice.

"It's… it's him, Mr. Lewis!" Mr. Lewis thinks I ran from a relationship that would never have worked, which is kind of true, just not the way he thinks. So, when I say 'him,' Mr. Lewis's eyes widen, and he raises his eyebrows as he rushes to the food window that separates the kitchen and dining room. I hear the bell above the door announcing their entrance, and I close my eyes, gripping my order pad so tightly the edges bend in my sweaty hand.

"Why is he here?" I run my hand nervously over my head and nearly poke myself in the eye with the pencil stub I'm still clutching. He pries the order pad and pencil away from my hands.

"How would I know? He's your boyfriend," he whispers roughly as though Easton might hear him over the noise of the diner.

"Ex! Ex-boyfriend! And your burgers are burning!" I point to the grill where the patties sizzle and pop. As he curses and whips around, I ease to the opening, crouch low, and keeping my head mostly hidden, peeking over the edge.

He's bending over a menu sitting with Coop and Abby in a booth across the room and pointing to something while Abby pokes Coop playfully in the ribs and giggles. He's so perfect, dark hair, olive skin made darker from days spent on the baseball field no doubt, days of practice which have made his biceps and forearms firm and sculpted.

I let my eyes feast on him until he sits up straight; his brows crease as though he's deep in thought. His eyes scan the dining room, and he begins to turn in my direction. Shit! Does he sense me somehow, like I sensed him? We've always had that weird connection that bound us together since the first day in the library when I tutored him in English. I duck quickly and crouch all the way to the floor.

"Where is Vivian?" Julie's voice comes from above me where she stands at the food window. Mr. Lewis motions toward my hiding spot with his spatula. I look up and see her puzzled expression as she leans through the opening. "What are you doing? You have new customers in your section. I just seated them and gave them menus. They're probably ready to order drinks."

I shake my head, sweat beading on my forehead and hyperventilation quite probable. She shakes her head and looks at Mr. Lewis. "What's wrong with her?"

He plates a burger. "It's him," he says, giving her a look and shaking his head as he hustles the burger to her waiting hand.

"It's him? Him, him? The him you ran away from? Oh, Vivian, why's he here?" She looks back over her shoulder.

"Don't look at him!" I squeal.

Her head swivels back down to me. "You gotta go, now! I'll cover this. Go back to your apartment."

I look to Mr. Lewis who nods his agreement. "I'll send Alejandro to get you when the guy leaves."

"Thank you, Mr. Lewis, and you, too." I glance up at Julie who gives me a sympathy smile.

"Go." She shoos me with her hand and turns back to the dining room to deliver the burger.

Mr. Lewis reaches down his hand, and I take it, pulling myself to my feet. Then I do something incredibly stupid. I can't help myself; I need one more look. Slow-motion-movie-style, I turn around toward the booth where Easton sits.

He's looking right at me.

CHAPTER FOUR

I DASH FOR THE KITCHEN'S back door which leads to the storage room and lock it behind me. When my eyes adjust to the dark, I see Alejandro sleeping on the cot against the back wall in front of my salvation—the door leading outside. Great! Why did he put the cot in front of the door? Then I notice the boxes stacked in the open spot where the cot usually sits. The supply shipment from last night, freaking fabulous! Mr. Lewis must have moved the cot to make room for all of the boxes thinking Alejandro would unpack them today. I've got to wake him up if I'm going to get out that door.

I rush to the cot and shake his shoulder. "Alejandro, get up! Wake up! I need out that door!" But he only groans and turns onto his side away from me. "Get up now!" I shove him hard. Nothing, no movement, nada. "Okay, Alejandro, you asked for this!" I haven't really used my powers since I made the lady change my name and birth year. I've been afraid that I'd attract Hoyt's attention, just like I did before, but this is an emergency.

I hear Julie's voice from the dining room, "Hey! You can't go in there!"

Then I hear Mr. Lewis, "Now listen, you gotta let her go, son!"

Someone is rattling the door. I stretch my hand out and blue light erupts from the center where a zigzag like lightning glows. "Sorry, Alejandro." I send a blast of energy at the cot which twists it around and slams it against the other wall.

Alejandro sits up in confusion, and a little fear crosses his face. "What the—"

"You were dreaming, Alejandro. The cot did not slam into the wall." I easily and quickly put the suggestion into his mind as I rush for the door. Just as I reach for the knob to freedom, I hear the door behind me fly open and hit the wall. I turn. He's behind me in the doorway four steps away with an unreadable expression. I send a blast toward the outside door, propelling it open, and then I bolt through it.

I'm rounding the corner of the diner when he catches me by the upper arm. Instinctively, I put out my right hand, palm up, but this is Easton. I could never hurt him. Protecting him is the whole reason I ran in the first place.

He's breathing heavily from the chase, his sea-water eyes full of some emotion I can't name. He grabs my hand and places it on his chest, over his heart, then he yanks me against him and wraps his arms around me. He crushes me against him as though he thinks I'll evaporate from his hands, and for one minute, I let myself forget— forget the fear I'll be his death, forget the fear I'll never know who I am, forget everything. I close my eyes and rest my head on his shoulder, breathing in his summer-night scent and letting him hold me against him.

"Vivian, I thought I'd never see you again." His voice is melting my bones and my resolve, so sweet and soft. Just as I lean all my weight against him, he jerks away, and I nearly fall. Holding my upper arms, he stands at arm's length and repeats, "I thought I'd never see you again." Except this time his voice isn't full of honey. It's most definitely anger. His body resonates tension; his jaw is clenched, his brow drawn together. Not even when Trista attacked me at prom did he look like this.

"You're here?! None of us even knew if you were alive!" His grip on me tightens then he drops his hands to his side and his chin to his chest. His eyes are closed, and he's inhaling deeply through his nose.

I don't know what to say, so I don't say anything. When he looks at me again, I realize the expression in his eyes earlier was disbelief. He had believed me dead. It never occurred to me he would think I'd been killed, but all this time, he'd been laboring under the idea that I was dead.

"Vivian, I thought... we *all* thought you were dead. You and Charlotte never came home." He shakes his head and looks past me, out into the parking lot and the July heat radiating from the asphalt.

"Hey! You leave her be, you hear!" Mr. Lewis rounds the corner carrying the sawed-off shotgun he keeps hidden in a cabinet under the register. He says it's a necessity for an all-night diner.

I step around Easton toward Mr. Lewis. "It's okay, sir. I think we"—I gesture to Easton—"need to talk."

"Talk in the storeroom where I can keep an eye on this one," he says in a gruff, grandfatherly tone, and I nod my head in agreement, but when I reach back for Easton's hand, he pulls it away from me. By now, Abby and Coop skid to a stop behind Mr. Lewis. They both stare, open-mouthed, and I can only make brief eye contact with them as I slink back into the storage room, feeling about as low as the gas gauge on my old clunker. Easton follows but stops next to Abby and Cooper. I hear him tell Coop to take Abby and find a hotel nearby, that he'll call him later. I don't have the heart to tell him he won't find a decent place within fifty miles. Mr. Lewis puts his arm around me and walks beside me into the storage room.

"I sent Alejandro's lazy ass inside to cook so you'll have privacy, but I want that door left open a little, you hear? Probably won't close anyway after he kicked it open!" He jerks his thumb over his shoulder to indicate Easton who's standing just outside. I see Cooper and Abby turn to go around the building, but Abby turns back and pulls her hand from Coop's. She shoulders past Easton and flings herself toward me, squeezing the breath from me in a surprisingly stout hug. She kisses my cheek and teary-eyed says, "How is this possible? Oh, V! I missed you so much." Then Coop gives me a weak smile and nod of his head before tugging Abby's hand.

"Come on. You can catch up later." He and Abby disappear toward the parking lot.

Mr. Lewis glares at Easton one last time, closes the back door, and then returns to the kitchen where he immediately begins to yell at Alejandro. Poor guy, he's having a rough day.

I close the door even though it will no longer latch. Easton won't look at me. He's pacing the floor between the boxes and the cot. He stops and looks at me, shakes his head, and resumes pacing. After about three of these stops and starts, I'm beginning to get mad myself. I left *for* him! He has no right to be this angry with me! Okay, maybe he does, but still! As I open my mouth, he finally stops pacing and looks at me.

"I waited, locked in your room—where you locked me—for hours! Even after Coop managed to get me out of your room, I waited. I searched for days, weeks, for any sign of you. You have no idea the hell I've been through, waiting, searching, praying that you'd turn up!"

"The hell you've been through? I've been on my own since that night! Living in one sleazy motel after another, working whenever I can to buy gas and canned soup so that I can keep you safe!" When I point my finger in his direction, I notice my palm is glowing. Taking deep, steadying breaths as he had earlier, I move to the cot and sit down. Calm. Get yourself under control, Vivian.

"What are you talking about? Safe from the people who kidnapped Charlotte? Is she here, too? With you?" It suddenly dawns on me that he doesn't know. He doesn't know she's dead.

"You don't know, do you?"

"No, Vivian, where you're concerned apparently I don't know anything." He huffs and throws up his hands.

I'm not sure I can even say it aloud. I close my eyes, willing the tears away, and see her as she looked in that van when she died, barely able to speak. The glass, the blood. And I know it's useless battling the emotions.

"She's dead, Easton. They killed her. *I* killed her by fighting them. He won, the man from my dreams, the same one who forced my mother to sacrifice herself for me. In the end I guess Aunt Charlotte did, too. When she took me in when I was five, she was destined to die. She just never knew it." I choke on the last word and sob into my hands. Then I feel his arm around me, pulling me into his embrace. I cling to his shirt front like a lifeline and cry like I've never cried before. In the last three months I haven't allowed myself to do this, to cry and cry till there're no more tears.

"Vivian, I didn't know. I'm sorry." I want so badly to let him take care of me, to be weak, but I can't. I still have to keep him safe, and I can't do that like this. He looks a little hurt when I pull away from him and stand.

"How did I not hear about this?"

"I don't—" Then it dawns on me. "They covered it up. Somehow they covered it all up." How could I not have thought of that sooner? My throat tightens again. "They disposed of her, of the evidence, and let everyone think we were both just missing." I turn away from him, from those eyes. I can't hurt him again; I have to force myself to push him away, and I know I could. It would be so easy to manipulate his mind, enter his thoughts and make him leave or better yet forget me entirely. Wouldn't that be the kindest way? But this is Easton. I can't do that to him.

When I feel him standing close behind me, I realize I'm just kidding myself. *Not* altering his mind is all for me because I can't stand the thought of him forgetting me.

"What do we do now?" Easton asks.

"I don't know, Easton." And for the first time in three months, that scares the hell out of me.

CHAPTER FIVE

I TELL EASTON EVERYTHING about that night at the park when my entire life changed—the men, the explosions, Hoyt's power. "It's like he could control the wind or something. He threw me around like a paper doll." I sit beside him on the cot and shrug. I've gone over all of this so many times in my head, still without finding any answers.

"Your turn." I face him. "How are you even here?" This seems like such an obvious first question but with my 'return from the dead' I haven't had the chance to ask it. "Sorry, that sounds a little harsh, but you know what I mean."

It's his turn to shrug. "Coop thought Abby and I needed to get out of town. We've both been so wrapped up in your disappearance that we haven't really been much fun to be around." He chuckles and shakes his head. "Coop said either we get in the car voluntarily or he'd hog tie us both and throw us in the back. So we took off, no real destination in mind." His brows draw together as he looks up at the ceiling like a fortune teller into a crystal ball.

"We've been on the road since Tuesday, wandering from town to town, looking at touristy junk—world's biggest ball of twine—stuff like that. But this morning, I volunteered to drive, and I don't know…" He trails off and looks into my eyes. I feel that familiar tingle, like he's looking right into my soul. "It's weird, Viv. I felt like something was sending me here, to you, I guess. When Abby started complaining about being hungry, I saw the sign for this place, and here we are."

He looks down to my hands where they rest in my lap and takes my right hand in his. I feel a jolt so powerful that I gasp. It's like the first time I ever touched him in Mrs. Crafton's room before we even knew each other's names. There's no denying it; a connection exists between us, a strange connection I don't understand.

"I've missed you so much." He leans in close, and I feel his breath on my face. I can't let him kiss me. I just can't. That will only make leaving him again so much harder. I'm about to pull away when Easton's phone rings. Saved by the bell! He hesitates to move.

"Answer it. It's probably Cooper," I say, hoping he doesn't notice my relief.

Without taking his eyes off of me, he digs the phone from his back pocket. This is my chance to distance myself from him, so I walk into the kitchen where Alejandro is wiping his face with a dirty kitchen towel. The buzz from the dining room tells me that we're really busy, and I feel totally guilty for abandoning poor Julie.

"Where you been, *chica*?" he asks while he grabs some plates from the shelf beside the grill. "We are busy! Get out there *rapido* and help Julie! Mr. Lewis had to leave, so she's alone."

I hear Easton telling Coop he'll call him right back, so I turn to the storage room.

"Coop says the only motel near here is about a half-mile down the road. Some nasty place that probably rents by the hour—his description, not mine." Smiling that tackle-me-to-the-ground grin, he puts the phone back into his pocket. I know exactly where he's talking about since that's where I live at the moment, but I really don't want to tell him that.

"So, guess this means you guys will have to be moving on?" I ask hopefully but deeply sad at the same time. His eyes narrow as he steps toward me.

"Ready to get rid of me so fast, huh?" He shakes his head and smirks. "Vivian, you and I have a lot to talk about. I'm still not sure I understand exactly why you feel the need to run from me or protect me for that matter, but I intend to find out because you and I are going to have a long talk tonight." Pulling out his phone again, he pushes the screen then puts it to his ear.

"Coop, rent some rooms. We're staying."

CHAPTER SIX

THE CUP CRASHED TO THE FLOOR spilling the strange blue liquid across the hearth stones where it steamed into the cracks. She felt her knees give as she buckled under the intensity of another wracking pain. It felt as though she would be torn in two. Her fists clenched the fabric of her nightshift. She gritted her teeth to keep from crying out, but when the next pain assaulted her, her hands clutched at her abdomen, and her scream echoed in the darkened kitchen. Rain slashed the window and whipped the branches of the oak tree violently against the glass.

Sweat beaded on her forehead and dampened the loose curls around her face though the room still held the chill of night. She breathed deeply in an attempt to think clearly. She had to wake Ethan. If she could wake him, he could go for Goody Smythe, the old midwife. The babe obviously had decided to make an early appearance. She made to rise again using the kitchen chair to pull herself up, but just as she reached her feet, pain seared through her, and she bent double, screaming, "Ethan! Ethan!"

She fell to the floor, curled on her side, grabbing her swollen belly. The door leading to the servants' quarters flew open and slammed against the wall where it rattled the pewter dishes lining the hutch as a young, breathless man clad only in knee-length breeches scanned the room, jerking his head from side to side to locate the girl.

"Virginia, what it is? Is it the babe?" Ethan, a free servant the master had hired right before Robert left for England, was the only person in the household who hadn't turned against her when her secret became obvious. From the moment Virginia had first seen Ethan sneaking books from the master's library, their bond had been sealed. He'd helped with her duties when he could escape his own, often drawing the wrath of Lord St. Clair for leaving his duties undone. By dim candlelight he read her tales of faraway lands where brave warriors were awarded a place in the stars while she sewed clothes for the babe, and she saved the choicest pastries and slices of pie for him, hiding the treats from Goody Crowe. He was also the only other person who knew of her relationship with Lord St. Clair's son. He'd become an invaluable friend, and a part of Virginia's heart wished she'd met him before she and Robert had begun their secret tryst. He rushed to her side and lifted her into his arms. She clung to his bare shoulders, sobbing now as the pain clenched her tightly in its clawed embrace.

"Get Goody Smythe, Ethan," Virginia panted. "Hurry! I fear the babe will beat her here!" When he turned toward the entrance to the servants' quarters to carry her to her bed, a voice boomed from the open doorway where rain now lashed inside, wetting the kitchen floor.

"What is going on in here? This screaming is disrupting my work! This is a crucial time, and I can't waste a night like this!" The master's thin, small frame stood silhouetted against the lightning flashing outside. His clothes were wet through, his gray hair plastered against his head.

"Lord St. Clair, Virginia's time has come. I must fetch Goody Smythe, the midwife!" Ethan, taller and work-hardened, towered over the man.

"You'll do no such thing! I'll not have that woman here. The villagers already question my experiments. If she is seen here, no amount of money will buy their silence! I'll be forced out of here, and I can't afford the interruption of starting over again when I'm so close to success!" He grabbed Ethan's arm and pushed him toward the door to the servants' quarters.

A hefty woman barred their way. Hands balled on her large hips, robe cinched around her beefy waist. Nightcap bobbing, she presented a formidable wall. Her angry face was evident even in the dim light of the kitchen. Cheeks quivering with outrage, she pointed toward Virginia where she moaned in Ethan's arms.

"The likes of her will never deliver that devil's spawn in this house!" She turned her beady, narrowed eyes on Lord St. Clair. "You should have turned her out when she began to show her sin, but you refused to even listen to me what with your experiments and dinners with the fancy folk!" She hustled her girth to the cup where it lay on the hearth and snatched it up in her hand. "For weeks she's been drinkin' a brew from that, that witch! I tried to find it to burn it proper and rid this house of her black magic, but she's hidden it well from me!" She threw the cup into the fire. "If you allow her to deliver that creature in here, we'll all be damned to Hell for her sin!" She moved to block the doorway once again.

"Goody Crowe, you will remove yourself from that doorway this instant! I remind you I am lord and master here, and my time has been wasted enough this night!"

"If you allow this, I'll leave, and I'll take the others with me. We'll tell all the villagers of this, and you'll be run out of here, your house burned! All your experiments ruined!" Though his face contorted in rage, St. Clair backed up a step at her threat.

Thunder clapped, swallowing the sound of Virginia's scream. Ethan turned toward the open doorway behind him and carried Virginia into the storm.

CHAPTER SEVEN

FIVE MORE MINUTES. My shift ends in five more minutes. The afternoon sun has heated the dining room to a sweltering temperature and my polyester uniform is sticky and damp on my back. For what seems like the hundredth time, I pass the booth where Easton, Abby, and Cooper have been staked out since earlier today.

After our little tete-a-tete in the storage room, Easton insisted on staying in the diner until my shift ended. Despite Julie's assurance that she could handle it and I should go with them to catch up, I stayed. Truth be told, I want to avoid the inevitable 'you gotta come back home' speech. Easton won't listen—my heart screams that— but I have to try. If he won't, I'll wait till he's asleep, then I'm gone again. The thought of it makes my stomach churn, and this heat is increasing my pre-hurl anxiety.

At 3:30 pm on the dot, Easton grabs my forearm as I pass the booth. "Shift's over, Vivian. No more stalling." Easton has already told Coop and Abby about the night Aunt Charlotte was killed. At least, I won't have to recap all that again.

"Let me get my bag." I pull away from him, head for the counter, and take off my apron. Julie takes the apron and hands me my bag. She gives me a sympathy smile, the kind you get right before the doctor diagnosis you have an unpronounceable disease that you will survive after some painful treatment.

"You gonna be okay? You don't have to go with them, ya know? I could get Alejandro to give 'em the boot, and you could hide at my place." She rubs my shoulder.

"Let's see five kids in a single-wide trailer or a night with the people I've hurt beyond measure... It's a tough decision." Julie's sweet, but I think I'd rather let Easton guilt me to death. I pretend to mull this over then return her weak smile and hug her across the counter. "Thanks, Julie, but I have to face them. Hey, do me a favor, though? Take my shift tomorrow? You're supposed to be off, but I'm afraid I might need more than one night to convince them I left for a good reason." And to get them to leave me here or escape them again, I mentally add.

Abby and Coop walk hand-in-hand to the door, and I'm so relieved that at least one of us has a good life. Easton introduced them at a bonfire last school year, and they hit it off until Dillenger and Trista got in the way. I guess Coop took care of that after prom, though. Wow! That seems so long ago—a lifetime ago, when my biggest issue was a bitch with fake boobs and hair extensions. I took so much for granted.

I walk beside one of those people to the SUV, and he holds the door for me. His unsmiling face mirrors my own, and only Abby seems unaffected by the tension when we climb inside the SUV.

"V, I'm so excited to see you! We've got a million things to talk about! Like my new ride? Dad completely freaked when you disappeared, took some extreme parenting 101 class, and became totally obsessed with keeping me safe from the boogeymen out there!" She giggles and leans forward between the front seats while Easton starts the car. "Said my Mustang was unsafe for a young girl. So, where do you live? Let's go to your house." Her face beams, and her blonde curls bounce in her pigtails.

Making a face as sour as the mood between Easton and me, I sigh. Truth time. Again. "You've already been there, actually." At the puzzled tilt of her head and Easton's crinkled brow, I turn and look out the window. Suddenly, I'm embarrassed, ashamed for them to see how I've lived these last few months. Aunt Charlotte and I never had any money. Our house was always run down, our furniture old, but we had a home, a real home, not a crappy motel room in a town where more people pass through in a day than live here all year.

I turn toward her. "I, well, I live in the motel where you're staying. I'm on the weekly plan, not the hourly one." Giving Coop a tight-lipped smile over Abby's shoulder, I almost choke on my own joke. Three sets of owl eyes stare back at me beneath raised brows.

Abby sputters, "Oh well, uh, okay." I've done the impossible. I've silenced Ab. I chuckle and shake my head when she leans into Coop's side in the backseat.

Clearing his throat, Easton says, "You must be tired."

As we pull away from the diner, blinding light obscures my vision. I close my eyes and reach for the dash. In my mind, I see a dark room, lit only by a bare bulb hanging from the ceiling. No sunlight, no sound save that of a continuous dripping. Metal pinches my wrists, and my arms ache behind my back. Damp cold chills the sweat on my temple. My heart pounds so loudly I think it might explode. A sliver of light, a door, opens above me at the top of the stairs. I whimper.

CHAPTER EIGHT

THEN IT'S OVER. I gasp loudly and jerk back as though I can get away from the image, the feeling.

"Vivian! What is it? What happened?" Easton grips my arm. I see his hand through white-tunneled vision, but I can't release my hold on the dash where my palm glows blue and the expensive leather begins to heat. He leans close, wrapping his arm around my shoulders. My breathing begins to calm, and as I close my eyes, I'm able to release the dash. Some things don't change. Easton has always been able to calm me. Any storm of emotion melts away when he's close to me.

"Are you okay?" His blue-green eyes soothe me in an unexplainable way. I flinch when his hand swipes across my cheek. Tears? I wipe my eyes in confusion. "What was that? You were gone for a second." He puts his hands up, reaching for an explanation. "You were here—with us—but your mind wasn't. What did you see?"

"I don't know? A room, dark and cold. I was there somehow, handcuffed, and I was... was so afraid, Easton. I think I was inside someone's head, and that person was scared, scared of someone."

Exchanging worried looks with the backseat, Easton asks, "Was this person near here? You think you could find that room?"

"Near, I think; I don't know. That's never happened before." Pulling out the ponytail holder that's kept my hair in place all day and slipping it on my wrist, I run my hands through my hair, my nervous habit.

"Whatcha wanna do here, Viv?" Coop's slow drawl comes from the backseat. When I look at him, I still see the huge teddy bear he was months ago holding the hand of my closest (a.k.a. only) friend, and I'm really glad they have each other. I'm not jealous. I'm not jealous a bit that they have a normal relationship, that they get to go out on actual dates, hold hands, not be afraid a crazy mutant man with obsidian eyes will kill the people they love. Nope, not jealous one little bit. Did I mention how often I lie to myself lately?

"We leave, Coop. I don't even know what or who that was, so I have no idea what I'm supposed to do about it." I pretend it was nothing, like I'm not completely freaked out, so that they don't ask any more questions I can't answer. Later, when I'm alone, I'll try to figure this out.

About five minutes later we park in front of room 115 at the Shady Rest motel, a total contradiction because there's not a tree in a one-mile radius, and it's impossible to rest when you're worried that the mice will unite to carry away your bed in the middle of the night. All of the doors of this five-star crap hole face outside toward the highway. Besides an empty, cracked pool, an ice machine and a soda machine sit near the office and surprisingly still work despite their faded appearance.

"Which one's your room, V?" Abby asks, leaning between the seats again.

"I'm down there, room 121." I point to the right where my beater car sits peeling and rusting in the sun.

"That your car? Where's your Aunt Charlotte's car?" she asks.

"I traded it to help cover my tracks. Nice, huh?" I try unsuccessfully to smile. Abby looks down. I have a feeling she's guilt-trippin' right now about the $50,000 SUV her dad bought her to keep his baby girl safe. But it's not her fault; none of this is anyone's fault but my own. I put my hand on her shoulder.

"It's not as bad as it seems, Ab. I've seen and done things I might never have had the chance to. It's okay, really, Abby." I duck my head down so that we are eye level. "Hey, I've got some great vintage clothes I bought in a little secondhand store a couple of towns over. Wanna go see?" Abby's love of fashion overrides her guilt, and she smiles.

"Yeah, let's go. The guys can get us some ice and sodas." She quickly pecks Coop on the cheek and slides out. I feel Easton's eyes on me as I get out and drag my tired body to my little home sweet home while trying to hold the smile that I don't really feel.

* * *

"Oh, I love this one!" Abby screeches for the third time. She's tried several tops from my limited wardrobe, and even though we aren't the same size, I must admit she looks better than I do in them. She definitely fills them out. The neckline of the red and blue gingham falls exactly where it should on her. Three inches shorter but with way more curves, Abby radiates cute, at least in my eyes and apparently in Coop's, too, judging by his expression when I open the door to their knock.

"Dang, girl!" He wolf whistles loudly. He and Easton are carrying several sodas and a full ice bucket that I assume came from one of the rooms they rented. Abby preens in front of the dresser mirror, one of the few pieces of furniture in the room, while I lay crossways on the bed where I've watched her raid my scant wardrobe. Shirts are thrown haphazardly on the bed in front of me, carnage from her fashion rampage.

"You like?" She saunters over to Coop, tosses the sodas he's carrying toward Easton, pushes him down in the only chair where she plops down on his lap, and wraps her arms around his neck.

"No, sunshine, I love it," he says, echoing her earlier statement and ogling the cleavage pushing its way into his face.

"Maybe I should buy this one from Viv. Whatcha think?" She squeezes him tighter, enhancing her assets, then giggles.

"I think I'm going to be sick." I pretend to gag as a grinning Easton closes the door behind him and puts the sodas and ice bucket on the dresser. When they begin to kiss as though we aren't in the same room, I get up to straighten up the room a little and to avoid looking in their direction. Easton and I lock eyes in the mirror, and he clears his throat.

"Come on, you two, enough of that junk." He sounds harsher than he probably intended. Coop's grin is huge when they pull apart.

"Sorry, buddy, I know we promised, but it's not my fault." He holds up his hands in surrender. "I'm only human. When my girl looks this good, I can't be held accountable for my actions."

Abby giggles again. "It's V's fault. It's her shirt."

"Yeah, but it sure doesn't look like that on me. Keep it, Abby. Enjoy." I gather some clothes for myself and head to the cupboard-size bathroom. "I need a shower." I finally look in Easton's direction where he stands awkwardly, hands in his pockets, beside the door. "Make yourselves at home. Remote's on the table. If you're lucky, the tv will be having a good day and will actually come on."

I gesture toward the tiny set where it's perched on the edge of the dresser and nearly trip over my feet to get to the bathroom and away from them all. Maybe it's because I've been alone for months, but I feel totally uncomfortable. Most likely it's because I want to throw myself into Easton's arms and beg him to kiss me like that.

After the shower I'm more composed, as though I might actually be able to control my raging emotions and not attack Easton. After shoving my dirty underwear into my laundry bag, I rehang my uniform and spray it with fabric freshener so that I won't be too rank the next time I need it.

"Gross, V," Abby says from the bed where she, Coop, and Easton sit watching a game show.

"I know, but I can't wash it every day." By the way her nose is squished up and the twist of her lips, I can tell she thinks she could never wear a dirty uniform day after day, and three months ago, I would've had the same disgusted expression.

I grab a soda from the dresser top and pretend I can't feel three pairs of eyes following my movements. They gawk like I'm some unidentified animal on exhibit at the zoo, but then again, maybe I am.

"Let's take a walk, Vivian." Easton rises from the bed and moves in my direction.

"Sure, I'll show you around town. It'll take about five minutes." He smiles, a genuine smile, and opens the door.

"I try to give these two an hour of alone time every day since we started this adventure, so I guess we'll just have to find something else to do, huh? It'll be tough, but I can think of something." He puts his hand on my back and propels me forward; Coop's laughter follows us out of the door.

CHAPTER NINE

THE SUN SINKS A LITTLE LOWER in the sky, taking a lot of the day's heat with it. Summer nights here aren't like back home. The humidity doesn't make you feel miserable, and the mosquitoes don't try to turn you into a corpse. It's actually kind of pleasant, and I long even more for Aunt Charlotte's blackberry cobbler and the talks we used to have on the front porch swing.

I've barely said two words since leaving Abby and Coop to snuggle or do any number of things that I don't want to think about. Easton, on the other hand, hasn't stopped talking. The entire walk he's been trying to convince me that I need to leave when they do.

Behind the motel, the old town begins. A lot of it is semi-abandoned, a scattering of homes still inhabited and a few small businesses struggling for life. It's like a ghost town really. We did pass one house where two small girls were swinging on an old tire hung from a tree near their house, making me miss my old life, and I'm thinking of those two when I notice some clouds beginning to gather above us.

"You're not listening again, Vivian. Have you heard *anything* I've been saying?" Easton snaps my attention to his face.

"Uh... no, sorry. I was looking at those clouds." I point up. "Think it might rain on us."

"Stop." He pulls me to a stop on the edge of the old town square. The few shops still alive have been closed up by this time, so it's just us. "Just stop, Viv. You are not avoiding this anymore." His voice is unyielding.

"Avoiding what, Easton? Avoid lying to you by telling you I'm going home again? Avoid thinking about how screwed up all of this is? Avoid wishing we could be like Abby and Cooper?" Sighing, I turn away and blink back tears.

"I want more than anything to climb in that SUV and leave with you guys. It would be heaven not to worry about anything except what to wear my first day back to school. But even if I go back with you, I'll never have that. Technically, I'm still a minor. I won't be eighteen till spring, so I can't even live in my old house alone. I can't support myself and go back to school. Oh! And let's not forget an insane murderer will find you, Abby, and Cooper and kill you because I won't join him." Light thunder sounds as more clouds gather.

"Then I'll stay with you, Vivian. I'm not leaving when Cooper and Abby go," he says firmly.

I spin around. His aqua eyes are stern, his jaw set. "No, you're not. I've told you, you aren't safe as long as you're with me. If Hoyt hasn't come for you in all this time, then you'll be safe again when you're gone!" My hands are fixed at my sides.

"We've already been over this. I don't care! Now that I know you're alive, I'm not going anywhere! And don't even think about locking me in a room again!" He's pointing at me. "I will always find you, Viv."

"Yeah, so will *he*!" I push him in the chest before I realize what I'm doing. He flies backward about ten feet and lands on his back just as the clouds open up.

"Easton! Please be okay!" I rush to his side and drop to my knees. He's blinking his eyes open, struggling to sit up and to catch the breath that I've knocked from him. "I'm so sorry. I didn't mean to!" I run my hands over his chest and arms, assessing if I've hurt him. "See, Easton. You're not even safe from me!" I try to jump up, but he grabs my arm, pulling me back down beside him.

Keeping a firm grip on me, he says, "This is why I should stay with you."

And it happens. The moment I've dreaded since I saw him walking across that parking lot earlier today. In a deserted town square where rain falls steadily, his lips press urgently against mine, and I'm powerless to stop him.

His hands move to my face as he deepens the kiss. His soft, full lips move over mine again and again. I taste the warm rain and the sweetness of his mouth. When he pulls away at last, I can only blink at his perfect face, spotlighted by my luminous eyes.

He smirks in victory, knowing I had been avoiding kissing him. "It's going to be dark soon. We should go." He looks up with his rain-slicked face. "Why does this usually seem to happen when we kiss?"

"Why... why did... you do that?" I'm stammering. One stupid kiss, and I'm a mess! Some independent woman I am!

"Because you wouldn't listen, so" — he shrugs and looks back at me with those damn eyes — "I had to show you."

And I'm reminded of Aunt Charlotte's 'if you can't listen you can feel speech' that I must have heard a million times whenever I wouldn't do what she'd told me to do. She inevitably turned out to be right. I had to feel the consequences of my choices and am I ever feelin' them right now!

As he pulls me to my feet, my brain finally begins to work again. I push the wet hair out of my face. "You know, it would be so easy to brainjack you, make you want to leave, forget all about me." I'm fairly certain I *could* accomplish all of this — if I wanted to, that is.

He jerks me under an old store awning that only has a few holes in the striped canvas while the rain continues to fall from a darkening sky. "Do it then!" His voice is unyielding, brokering no argument.

I stumble against him. "Do what?"

"Do what you said you could. Blank my memory of you and make me leave here." He puts my hands on his face. "Come on. You're so tough. Let's see it."

Mouth opening and closing like a dying goldfish, I squeak out, "I... I can! I will!"

"Alright, do it!" Tension radiates from his body.

I close my eyes and see into his mind. He's trying to keep it empty, but I can hear a tiny voice that I'm sure he doesn't want me to hear. *Don't do it, Vivian. I love you.*

And this is why I can't bring myself to fulfill my boast. I want this. I want him to love me. It feels right, like we've loved each other forever, and without meaning to, I accidentally put a thought into his head, a picture actually, a wicked, shocking picture caused by just touching him. My glowing eyes flash open as I yank my hands from his face. His laugh heats me even more, and my face feels hot with embarrassment.

"Told you that you couldn't do it," he says pulling me against his chest where I put up a weak resistance and absolutely cannot meet his eyes. "In fact, I'd say that was pretty much the opposite. Wouldn't you agree, babe?" Easton's hand beneath my chin forces me to meet his intense gaze. "I won't have any problem recreating that picture if you want me to." He leans toward me, and I'm so tired of fighting my feelings for him. What the heck! I might as well enjoy his nearness for as long as I can before I take off again because no matter what, I *will* leave him behind again. Until then, I'll let him think he's won.

"I might just let you," I whisper as I tug his head to mine and kiss him like there's no tomorrow.

CHAPTER TEN

THE RAIN HAS SLOWED TO A DRIZZLE, and since we're already soaked we take the long way back to the motel. We're walking through a section of town I've never seen. Some of the houses here are not as run down as many of the others in town. The area close to the motel and truck stop must be the worst part of town.

A few street lights line the street here, and most of the houses are lit from within. I imagine the families inside sitting down to dinner. Maybe if I stay longer I could find a little house here to rent. The thought of staying has crossed my mind. I know I'm on this quest to find my father, but of all of my stops, I've been happiest here. Yeah, it's a nowhere town and a dead-end job, but the people I've met have become important to me. And maybe a dead-end job is exactly what I need right now, no thinking required. This would be the perfect hiding place, too, off the map, off the radar.

"What are you thinkin' about?" Easton pulls me back to reality.

"Oh, I don't know. Nothing. Everything." At his exasperated expression, I say, "Actually, I was wondering if I shouldn't plan on staying here for a little while." When he arches his left eyebrow nearly into his shaggy hair, I rush on. "I don't mind waitressing. It's tiring, but the money's the best I've made so far. Julie's great, and Mr. Lewis—"

Without warning, a blinding light bursts behind my eyes, and my knees buckle. Just like earlier today in the SUV, I'm no longer with

Easton. Once again, I see darkness, hear dripping, feel the damp cold, colder now than before. It seeps from the floor where my head rests, my cheek pressed against the concrete. My wrists and arms still ache but are no longer bound. I use them to push myself up, but I slam back down when my shaking arms refuse to support me, and my head smacks the floor with a stomach-turning thud.

* * *

"Vivian, V, wake up please!" Abby's face slowly comes into focus. "Oh, thank goodness! She's opening her eyes."

A cold wash cloth presses against my forehead; another rests on the back of my neck. "Ab, what happened?" My voice is strained, and I'm completely drained. Easton's face looms above mine, dark brows drawn together.

"It happened again, like this afternoon except this time you've been out for over an hour." He digs his fingers into his disheveled hair, a helpless expression on his handsome face.

Abby takes the rag from my forehead and bathes my heated cheeks. "Easton called us, and when we finally found you two, you were like, well, like this. Not exactly like this, like you were a second ago. Totally unconscious." Coop moves to stand behind Abby dropping his hand reassuringly on her shoulder.

"What did you see this time?" Easton asks, helping me to sit up.

"More of the same room, but this time, I was so tired." My eyes close and I inhale deeply as that same wave of exhaustion sweeps through me. I manage to tug open my eyes again and see their worried expressions, but keeping them open proves more difficult than walking on water. My entire body is zapped, and all I want is to sleep, but Easton is having none of it.

"Vivian, you need to open your eyes." Fear makes his voice severe and demanding.

"I can't. I'm just so… please let me sleep," I beg, eyes sliding closed again.

"You guys go. I'll stay with her." His melodic voice rumbles against my back where I'm slumped against him. Snuggling deeper into his arms, I feel safe for the first time in forever as I drop off into sleep.

* * *

Coffee, strong coffee, something sugary sweet, and Easton—not the worst of smells to wake up to.

The bed bounces slightly as he shifts his weight. His warm arm brushes my ear as he settles back against the headboard. When he turns to look at me, his relief is evident in the soft expression of his eyes. His hair sticks up as though he hasn't slept or at least not slept well.

"Finally! You're awake. Another half hour and I was going to take you to the emergency room."

The cottony thickness of my tongue fills my mouth. I swallow but that doesn't help. I move to sit, and Easton puts his arm behind me to ease me up. I point to the insulated coffee cup where it sits on the bedside table.

As he hands it to me, he says, "I can get you something else if you want me to. Coop brought this and some donuts by about ten minutes ago. You've been out since around 8:00 last night. When you still hadn't woken up at midnight, I wanted to take you to the hospital then, but Coop and Abby thought that might not be the best move—too many questions. I told them if you didn't wake up by 8:00 this morning, I was taking you regardless of what they thought."

While I sip the coffee, I glance down at the cover someone has thrown over my lower body. I try to smooth my hair and realize what a tangled mess it is. Shaking my head, I hand Easton the cup with the diner's logo printed on the side.

"You've been here all night? Have you slept at all?" The slight, dark crescents under his blue-green eyes and his rumpled clothes testify to his all-night vigil with me.

"I slept a little, dozed off for a couple of hours, but you yelled in your sleep, and I couldn't go back to sleep after that." He shrugs and looks away, slightly embarrassed. "I didn't know what to do, babe. I was scared that you'd never open your eyes again, that I'd lose you after I just got you back." His cheeks pink, he finally meets my eyes and grins his sinful grin. "And I slept on top of the covers since Abby insisted on making you more comfortable." He nods his head in the direction of the blanket, and for the first time, I realize

I'm not wearing any pants. Now, it's my turn to blush as I feel the heat crawl up my neck to my face.

"Don't worry. I didn't peak" —he leans close to me—"not more than once or twice." Pulling back, I cover my mouth with my hand. I'm not about to kiss his perfect lips with my dragon breath. Undaunted, he lifts one eyebrow and pulls my hand away.

"But I have morning breath," I weakly protest but make no move to escape him.

"So do I," he whispers, and when his lips meet mine, I forget to breathe. When he eases me back against the pillows, I forget to think. All I can do is feel his warmth, his strength.

When he kisses the spot beneath my ear and slides his hand along my hip, I almost forget I have to leave again soon—almost. In the back of my mind, that nagging, sensible voice reminds me that I'll never have a real life with this boy. I'll always be a danger to him as long as Hoyt is still out there. Telling myself to just enjoy him while he's here won't work forever. I have to face reality, and *this* is not reality. It's too wonderful. Reality isn't, at least not my reality.

Breathless and wanting to punch my stupid, responsible face, I move to stop him. His lips tickle the pulse at the base of my neck. "Easton, we need to talk."

He squeezes my hip and returns his attention to my lips. Between kisses, I try again to regain control of both of our hormone-overloaded senses. "Easton, seriously, we need to talk about our future." Or lack of.

Inches from my face, so close his labored breath tickles across my cheek, he looks into my eyes, and a tug pulls on my memory. I swear I've seen that same intense look a million times before now, before this moment. A sensation like eternity shoots through me, and judging by his expression, he senses it, too, almost like déjà vu.

A booming knock on the door breaks the mood, causing us both to jump and look toward the door like its sprouted horns and fangs.

"Hey! It's pourin' out here, Easton. Let us in!" Coop's enormous voice penetrates my foggy brain.

With a sigh, Easton says, "Guess we could ignore them."

"I think their timing might actually be pretty good." I smile sheepishly, part of me relieved to postpone our talk and our make-out session.

He huffs and shakes his head. "Vivian, I swear. Sometimes you make me crazy." He pulls away from me and clears his throat. I follow his gaze to find the blanket is no longer covering my legs but is instead wadded around my knees and ankles. My pink-striped undies are in full view. I don't know what's more embarrassing, the panties or my legs that need shaving.

Gasping, I reach for it, but he beats me to it and pulls it up to my chin, effectively tucking me in burrito-style. Laughing, he moves from the bed toward the door but stops with his hand on the knob.

"Pink is definitely your color, babe." When he winks, I toss a pillow (which he catches too easily) at him. He's still laughing when he opens the door to a dripping Cooper and Abby who look none too happy to have been kept waiting.

"What's so funny?" Abby snarls. I'd forgotten how cranky she can be before noon.

Easton pauses to glance back at me over his shoulder and wink. "Vivian and I were discussing fashion, right babe?" My cheeks flame.

When he calls me that, I melt inside. Maybe it's the mortification talking, but that simple, one-syllable word makes tiny starbursts of goofy sappiness explode in me. That word makes me supremely happy, like I've eaten a bag of sugar-coated candy topped with ice cream and syrup, and I'm ridin' a sweet high.

"What are you talkin' about? I'm, like, soaked here." Abby pushes Eaton's shoulder and shoves past him, trailing Cooper behind her.

"Nothing, not important. Rain again?" Easton closes the door behind Cooper as he slogs in and plops down in the only chair.

"Ya think?" Abby's sarcasm only makes Easton smile. She gathers her soggy hair and wraps my ponytail holder that she picks up from the dresser around it.

"We, uh, didn't notice." He grins at me, and I can't help but smile and drop my gaze briefly to my lap.

Abby looks between us like she's watching a tennis match then says, "Hm, I wonder why." Then she smiles, too, finally.

"Rain just started outta nowhere about ten minutes ago. Not a cloud in the sky then poof! It's pouring!" Coop grabs a donut from the box on the bedside table.

"We were going to get breakfast and thought we'd check on V first." Abby snatches Coop's partially eaten donut, tears off a piece, and pops it in her mouth before plopping on the bed beside me. She makes a face. "Ew, these are not very good. Where'd they come from?" she asks, looking at Easton.

He points to Coop. "Ask him. He brought them by early this morning."

Cooper takes another. "Tastes okay to me." He shrugs. "Got 'em at the diner where Vivian works."

"Mr. Lewis makes them every morning," I reply, seizing the donut from Abby and taking a bite. Something's off, not quite right. "Was Mr. Lewis there this morning, Cooper?"

"Is that the old guy we saw yesterday with the gun?" At my nod, he continues, "Nope, don't think so. Just that same waitress and some pissed off Mexican guy."

Strange. In all the time I've been here, I've never known Mr. Lewis to miss one morning of donut making. He told me he'd always wanted to be a baker, make pies, cakes, cookies instead of slinging greasy burgers and fries. During the overnight hours when he's the only person there, he bakes. He makes all of the pastries we serve, every slice of pie or cake. It's his specialty and his passion—the one thing he really loves doing.

"What is it, V? You've got that look on your face? You having another"—Abby flounders for a word—"episode thingy?"

"No, I'm just worried. Mr. Lewis should be there. Alejandro says he left early yesterday, and now he didn't make the donuts. I should go to the diner and see if he's sick or something." Holding the blanket around my waist, I swing my legs over the side of the bed.

"He's just your boss. What's the big deal if he doesn't make the donuts? Maybe he just took a day off," Abby says sitting up.

"He's more than that, and he *never* takes a day off, Ab." Her nonchalance irritates me a little. Abby has no idea how truly important Mr. Lewis has become to me. "He gave me a job and a place to stay when I was desperate. He doesn't have a wife or kids, no one to take care of him if he's sick. I need to check on him." Grabbing some clothes, I head to the bathroom as Easton closes the short distance between us. His hand keeps me from closing the bathroom door behind me.

"Hey don't go over there till I get back. I'm gonna go shower, and I want you to wait for me to go with you. I've got a weird feeling, Vivian." I smooth his crinkled brow with my fingers.

"I'll wait." He raises his eyebrows. "I promise."

In less than twenty minutes Easton and I are walking into the diner. The gloomy weather makes the diner seem warm, cozy even, but one look at Julie's face where she stands behind the counter tells me that she's as worried as I am.

"I don't know, Vivian. I feel like something's wrong." She's wrapping flatware in paper napkins in preparation for the lunch crowd. "Mr. Lewis hasn't missed a day in the two years I've been working here."

"Well, has anyone spoken to him?" I pick up a fork, spoon, and knife and hand them to her while she smooths a large, paper napkin.

"No, that's the really strange part! I can't imagine he wouldn't call Alejandro. He's been here longer than any of us, and Mr. Lewis trusts him to do a good job, but Alejandro told me he hasn't heard from him either. Mr. Lewis was supposed to be back for the night shift." She stops folding and pins me with a sick expression. "Alejandro had to close the diner overnight. Vivian, I think something really bad has happened. He's not a young man. What if he's had a heart attack or something?"

"I know, Julie. I feel the same way. Do you know where Mr. Lewis lives? Easton and I can go check on him." I glance over at Easton where he sits on a stool next to me.

He nods and says, "Where's his house?"

Between Alejandro and Julie, we manage to come up with at least a street name here in town and the general vicinity. As we're buckling up in the SUV, I'm thinking how sad it is that we don't know his house number. This man who supports us all, has given us all the semblance of stability and a family—a work one anyway—and *none* of us knows where he lives.

"Put the street into the GPS." Easton starts the engine and pulls me from my thoughts.

The GPS's robotic voice reminds me of Aunt Charlotte's kidnapping, which reminds me of how epically I failed her. I vow to take care of Mr. Lewis if he's sick or hurt.

As the GPS navigates us past the old town square, Easton says, "Hey, we weren't far from here last night when you had your"—he looks at me for a term for this newest freak show trick his weird girlfriend can do, but I just raise my brows as if to say 'this one's all yours' — "Your vision."

"You have arrived at your destination," the GPS announces as we emerge onto a residential street, a very familiar residential street. A tingle dances along my arm and into my hand. The clinch in Easton's jaw and the quick narrowing of his eyes tell me he recognizes it, too. This is the exact street where I had my vision last night.

CHAPTER ELEVEN

"VIVIAN?" EASTON BEGINS to say exactly what I'm thinking.

"Yeah, it is, Easton." I already fear the worst.

"You don't think the person, the one you keep seeing could be—" I nod my head, not wanting to hear it said aloud.

"Let's just see if we can figure out which house is his."

"Do you recognize his vehicle?" Easton moves slowly down the street, giving me a chance to glance at the cars.

"No, I've never really paid attention to what he drives. All of the employees park around back, but I always walk, so I have no idea." I listen for brain activity. I've never actually heard anyone's thoughts from inside of a house, but it's worth a try. Nothing. I have all this power, power I don't want, and none of it is helpful right now.

"Maybe we'll get lucky, and one of the mailboxes will have his name." To better see the names, he rolls down the tinted windows, letting in the humid air. Though the rain has stopped, the sky is darkening for another round, and the dancing lightning only fuels my unease.

"There!" He points to a surprisingly large, brick house. Red and white geraniums adorn a covered porch and well-trimmed bushes line the driveway. Mr. Lewis never ceases to amaze me. He works all night, and sometimes most of the day, but still he has the prettiest house in town. Well, maybe that's not saying much considering the rest of the houses in town.

We pull into the drive, get out, and cautiously approach the front door. My body involuntarily reacts to the uncertainty of what we'll find inside. Easton tries the knob.

"Locked, but I think we have a key." He takes my right hand in his and turns it palm up. He skims his thumb down the center where the blue, lightning-like line glows brightly.

"What are you doing?"

"Remember that little stunt you pulled to lock me in your room? You're gonna repeat it small scale and sort of in reverse."

"Why don't I just send a blast and knock it down?"

"Neighbors might hear if any are home. Babe, you gotta start thinkin' like a superhero." He winks and puts my hand against the wooden frame near the knob. My vision becomes a narrow, white tunnel as my palm heats, causing the metal mechanism holding the lock in place to glow. Concentrating, trying not to melt the entire knob and pinpoint only the locking bar, I close my eyes until finally Easton leans down beside my ear and whispers, "Okay, think that might be it."

When I open my eyes, I see the painted wood all around the knob and frame is brittle and black. Great. I've charred the door instead of melting the lock, which still glows orange.

"What do you mean? The lock's not melted," I snap, angry because I couldn't accomplish such a simple task.

"Yeah, but now we can do this." He glances around then pushes hard against the door with his shoulder. The fragile, extra-crispy wood around the locking bar gives way with a crunch, and we're in.

"Gotta work on that." Easton sweep me inside with his arm behind my back.

"How will we ever explain this to Mr. Lewis when we see him?" I squint to see Easton's face in the dark entryway.

"I think 'if' might be a better word." Easton pulls his cell out and holds it high to shine the lighted surface around the room.

The room is in complete disarray. Chairs and end tables are overturned. The television lies flat on the floor. Easton's right. The signs of a struggle are exactly like I've seen on a million cop shows. Something bad happened here, putting me immediately on def-con five alert.

"I don't understand. Why trash the place then lock the door behind you?"

Easton shakes his head. "I don't know. Keep out nosey neighbors?"

"Let's look for Mr. Lewis." I begin to lead the way, but Easton grabs my arm and pulls me behind him.

"Really? Easton, I just barbequed a door. It's very gallant of you, but I should be protecting you. Superhero, remember?" I don't want to bruise his ego, but seriously.

Undaunted, he continues in the lead anyway, phone held high. Room by room, we search without success. The other rooms aren't torn apart like the living room, but they're all as equally, eerily silent and empty. Mr. Lewis is nowhere to be found, but I can't shake the suspicion that something terrible happened here.

In the kitchen Easton stops and switches off his phone's light. Through the kitchen window the sky is dark and sinister. Lightning flashes, and thunder rolls, increasing my unease.

"There's no sign of him, Viv. What do you want to do now?" Easton asks, leaning against the counter.

"I guess we should just go back to the diner." Suddenly, a powerful jolt races through my body, the sensation strong enough to make me gasp. An image of a door flashes in my mind.

Easton clutches my shoulder. "What is it? What did you see?"

"I saw a door." I turn my head to the left. Not four feet away is the exact image in living color. I turn and face it head-on. "That door," I say pointing, then close the distance until I'm close enough to touch the knob.

Easton moves to stand behind me. Body thrumming with energy, eyes lighting the darkness enough to see Easton's face, I take a shaky breath to calm my racing heart.

"You sure you want to do this?" he asks. I nod and turn back to the door as I twist the knob, which opens easily.

The gray-white light from my eyes can't begin to penetrate the thick darkness. Holding out my blue palm, I create a glowing orb about the size of a grapefruit that shows a staircase leading down into the basement.

Easton reaches for his cell, but shaking my head, I take his hand and will the light orb into his palm. If I weren't so worried, I would laugh at the shock in his eyes.

"Can't believe that actually worked." I pull my hand away but leave the blue-white orb in his. I produce another orb and begin walking slowly down the stairs, descending into the damp coolness that smells slightly of wet earth. Images assault me like flashes from a strobe, still shots embedded into my memory. Before I reach midway on the staircase, the sound of dripping water annoys my ears and confirms what I fear to be true.

"Easton, I've been here before."

"I thought you didn't even know Mr. Lewis's address."

"Not physically." I meet his eyes over my shoulder in the unnatural glow of the orb.

Realization flashes across his face as my meaning dawns on him. "This is the place? Vivian, we should turn back, get out of here now." He reaches out, but I shake my head and pull away.

"No, I have to know." I step down another step.

"I think you already do." He shakes his head, but I turn away and continue down into the basement.

When my feet touch the concrete floor at the bottom, I am absolutely positive this is the place, the place from my visions. Near a corner, a dark, dried pool of deep crimson stains the floor. On the wall behind it, more blood spatters dot the surface in a macabre polka dot.

I kneel beside it and absorb my light orb back into myself. As soon as I do, more images assault me, except this time I'm no longer seeing through the victim's eyes.

I see his face, Mr. Lewis's face, where he kneels on this spot, bleeding from his nose, mouth, and a huge gash running down the side of his face and disappearing into his gray hair. It's the man I've come to care deeply for, the man who virtually saved my life when he gave me a job and a place to stay, and he's begging for death.

"Please, kill me. I'm an old man. Just kill me and be done with it. I've done what you commanded. I won't do anymore. I can't. I've gotten them here, all of them." His chin drops to his chest while his body slumps closer to the floor where his blood has already created a puddle around his knees.

"No, not quite. You haven't fulfilled your mission yet," says a second male voice from the foot of the stairs.

Mr. Lewis quickly snaps his head up and glares. Despite his injuries, he stiffens and rigidly straightens his spine, giving the man a defiant stare.

"I was out. They told me I was done. I've lived here quietly, running my diner for years. I haven't used my power in so long I wasn't sure I still could. Then you come along! I didn't like you before, and I sure as hell don't like you now! I did what you" —he sneers and curls up his split lip which bleeds anew— "commanded me to do in exchange for the safety of Julie and her family, and I'm through! So kill me if you're gonna! Your cowardly ass will have to do the rest yourself. I won't deliver her or *any* of them directly into your hands!"

Two long strides bring the man closer to Mr. Lewis. He presses the muzzle of a handgun into Mr. Lewis's temple and calmly says, "Oh, I think you already have."

A loud bang ends the vision, but the disembodied voice remains, "It won't be long now, my dear."

CHAPTER TWELVE

HOYT. HOYT'S HERE. In this town. He killed Mr. Lewis. "It was him, Easton, Hoyt Matthews, the man who kidnapped Aunt Charlotte."

Spinning around searching the close darkness, he asks, "Is he still here?"

"No." I run my hands through my hair. "I think I'd sense him." The last time I was close to him in the park, I felt connected to him. The only feeling I have right now is disgust at the vicious murder of Mr. Lewis.

"So, does he have Mr. Lewis then?" Easton steps closer to me and offers his hand to help me rise.

"No, Mr. Lewis is dead. I saw him killed." When I say it aloud my anger heightens until I'm shaking, my hand glowing like a sapphire lantern.

"I'm sorry, Vivian." Easton puts his arm around me, pulling me into his embrace. He flinches when I accidentally shock him, but he only holds me tighter.

"Babe, you have to calm down. You're in control, not him, and you had nothing to do with Mr. Lewis's death." He tries to reassure me, but he doesn't understand. How can he? He didn't see or hear what I did.

"You're wrong." I jerk out of his arms. "I did this! He was killed because of me! He was begging for death because he… he refused to deliver me—us—to Hoyt." I squeeze my eyes and try to take a deep breath.

"What? Us? Wait, did he know about your power? Did you tell him?"

"No, I would never tell him." I give a humorless laugh. "I didn't want to endanger him."

"I don't understand. Tell me what you saw." Easton's confusion draws his brows sharply together.

"I'll do better than that." I step to him and put my hands on either side of his face. "I'll show you."

I upload all of the images and the conversation directly into his brain. His eyes scan back and forth behind his closed lids, and he flinches at the memory of the gun shot. As I pull my hands away, he jerks his eyes open, an emotion I can't identify sits on his face.

"It sounds like Mr. Lewis knew way more than you thought he did."

"Yeah, Mr. Lewis knew Hoyt and was forced to use his *power*, whatever that means, to keep Julie safe. But to do what exactly?" I shake my head and throw up my hands.

"He said he wouldn't give 'her' or 'them' over to Hoyt. He must mean you, but it sounds to me like he was protecting us, too." He takes my hands in his.

I nod. "I think you're right. Hoyt wanted me to see this. He somehow planted this in my head. He wanted me to see him murder Mr. Lewis." My stomach lurches with the thought. I shouldn't be surprised by the lengths he'll go to, but actually seeing him kill someone and knowing I'm the cause makes me nauseous.

"Vivian, Mr. Lewis may not even be dead. This could all be a setup, planted, like you said, but not real. We could—"

But I hold up my hand, interrupting him. "It was real. I just know it. I sensed his pain and his fear. He's dead, and I'm the reason." Pulling my hand from his, I move past him and start up the stairs. "Come on. Let's get out of here." I can't bear the thought of him touching me when I know that every touch, every word puts him in danger.

After we're back in the SUV, Easton pauses, his hand hovering over the ignition. "What do you think Mr. Lewis meant when he said he wouldn't 'deliver' us to Hoyt?"

"I don't know, one of the many things I don't know. I'll just add it to my ever-growing list." Rain pounds the windows, and I gather my wet hair off of my face. As we pull away from Mr. Lewis's house,

I'm lost in thought, trying to come up with a plan to escape Hoyt and leave Easton, Abby, and Cooper safely behind. I don't notice that Easton is talking to me until he snaps his fingers near my face.

"Vivian, you still in there? Did you see something else?" he asks, mistaking my plotting for a vision.

"Sorry," I mumble, unable to look at his flawless face. I know what I need to do. As soon as they go to sleep, I have to run again.

CHAPTER THIRTEEN

THE STORM RAGED ALL AROUND HIM. His bare feet sloshed through ankle-deep water and mud as he carried her. Holding her close and hunching his shoulders around her to protect her from the ferocity of the storm, he dashed to the nearest outbuilding.

The large wooden structure stood less than ten feet from the kitchen door and was once attached to the main house, having been originally used as a smokehouse. However, Lord St. Clair, after declaring it perfect for his workroom, had filled it with strange devices of glass and metal. The fire that destroyed the front of the building and its connecting walkway had ignited the rumors, engulfing Lord St. Clair's experiments, and fueled the townspeople's superstitious fears. His refusal to reconnect the buildings caused even his loyal servants to gossip. Rumors of witchcraft and devil worship flourished, quieted only by the jingle of coin and the shine of gold. Though Ethan knew he would be severely punished, he pulled the unlatched door and pushed inside.

Huge glass cylinders in every shape and size lined the back wall; many were filled with shimmering liquids. Several lamps and candles sat haphazardly around the room, some on tables, others on shelves positioned high over cluttered work spaces. Their meager light created frightening shadows and brilliant reflections. Long, metal rods stretched to the ceiling and connected to the corners of a large work table in the cavernous center of the room. Strips of metal were spaced evenly across the wooden surface, some connecting to the rods. The viciousness of the storm caused droplets to zigzag down the rods.

Kicking aside empty wooden crates, Ethan made his way to the only clear surface in the room. He gently laid Virginia on the wood and metal table where she was dwarfed by its length.

"Virginia, what do I do?" Ethan leaned close and searched her storm-gray eyes for some answer. He found only agony and panic. As pain wracked her slight frame, she curled on her side, knees drawn to her chest, fingernails scoring her palms.

Rain pelted the open doorway, and rivulets snaked across the stone floor. His eyes skimmed the room for anything that might comfort her. Spotting an old coat and shirt tossed across a chair near the small fireplace, he rapidly crossed to them. His feet slipped on the smooth stone. When he returned to her side, he wadded the shirt, slid it under her head, and covered her shaking body with the coat.

"Should I fetch Goody Smythe?" he asked, taking her fisted hand in his own.

"No! Ethan, don't leave me! Tis too late!" She cried out and gripped his hand.

"You need her! I will return quickly. I swear it!" He turned to leave, but her desperate sob stilled him.

Tears mixed with her sweat and the rain still dampening her reddened cheeks. "I fear I'll not survive this, and I don't want to die alone."

He covered her cheek with his work-roughened hand and knelt down beside her. His turquoise eyes only inches from her face, he swore, "You will *not* die. I won't let you."

CHAPTER FOURTEEN

AS WE PULL INTO THE MOTEL PARKING LOT, I'm still in shock. Mr. Lewis, the man I trusted and cared about, knew Hoyt, the man I hate and despise. *And* he had some sort of powers that Hoyt forced him to use in exchange for not harming Julie. *And* he died rather than help Hoyt get to me, Easton, Abby, or Cooper. At least, that's what I think happened.

The relentless rain only increases my apprehension. I'm edgy because I know this is far from over, and we aren't safe. Tonight, while the others sleep, I'll throw some clothes in my backpack and go. Hopefully, Hoyt will follow and leave the others behind.

"Still no answer from Cooper or Abby." Easton clicks off his phone for the third time.

"I don't know about Coop, but that's really unusual for Abby." Whether intentional or not, I hear Easton's thoughts.

Just like Mr. Lewis.

Damn, he's right! I'd been too absorbed in my own plans of leaving to make the connection. One look at his face, and I'm grabbing for the door handle and scrambling out into the downpour. We sprint for the rooms Coop rented for the three of them. The door is ajar, the carpet soggy from rain. The interior is a replay of Mr. Lewis's living room—overturned chairs, upended table. Abby's purse lies on the floor near the bed; its contents are scattered, and her phone is smashed as though it's been stepped on. I pick up the expensive device and run my fingers over the cracked face. It momentarily flares to life, beeps once, and goes black again.

Easton frantically searches the room and the bathroom as though the three of them are playing some freakish game of hide-n-seek. Then he slams his fist into the wall, creating a huge hole. While his anger is obvious, my rage is tainted by fear for their safety.

"Easton, I'm so sorry." I did this as surely as if I'd kidnapped them myself. Involuntarily, tears escape and trail down my cheeks. My throat tightens, and I turn away from him. I can't bring myself to look at him, knowing his fury is my fault. I put that expression on his face by not running the first moment I had a chance, too caught up in enjoying the moment, his touch, his kiss. I didn't recognize the danger that was right in front of me.

His hand on my back makes me flinch and sob in earnest. My shoulders shake beneath his hand. "Vivian, this isn't your fault. Charlotte, Mr. Lewis, even your mom, none of it is your fault. He's insane, Viv, and he has some kind of support backing him. You can't possibly outrun that."

Hearing his concern for me makes me snap. I spin around, throwing my hands into the air. I can't take his kindness when I know I'm the cause of so much.

"Easton, stop being so damn sweet about this! Be angry with me! This is all happening because of me! They might DIE because this... this psycho is after me!"

Judging by the tight line of his mouth and the tilt of his brows, I think he might have listened and given me what I just asked for. Grabbing my upper arms, he gives a little shake. "You want me to be angry at you? You want me to be pissed because some crazy bastard is after you? How can you control that? You didn't create any of this. He did! He kidnapped Charlotte, Mr. Lewis, and maybe Abby, and Coop. Not you! I'm sick of hearing you blame yourself. This guilt you have is really startin' to wear on me *and* it's startin' to sound a whole lot like self-pity!" He pulls me into a strong embrace, wrapping his arms around me. This is not a gentle, 'everything's gonna be okay' hug; it's the 'we'll survive this shit together' variety. His fierce emotions flow into me, and I know he is purposely letting me into his mind. He's willing me his strength, determination, and optimism.

When he pulls away from me, I'm stronger, a little shocked, but stronger nonetheless. Why is he always rational? And why is he always right? I have been feeling guilt and pity.

His anger is draining away, and he looks a little surprised and sheepish. "Sorry, babe, I just"—he sighs and stares at the wet, brown rug—"I love you."

It's the first time he's said the words aloud since we were reunited, and that phrase is the very reason he's so right.

"Don't be sorry, Easton. Everything you said is true. It's time to stop blaming and start fighting back."

He closes his eyes for a second, and relief replaces worry. He's smiling when he looks back at me and squeezes my hands. "Thank God! I was afraid you were about to vaporize my ass."

"Now that would truly be a waste." I allow a small grin to escape before turning serious again. "Let's go back to my room. I've got a feeling Hoyt will be contacting me—us—soon."

CHAPTER FIFTEEN

THE RING OF EASTON'S CELL makes us both jump. After leaving the empty room where Coop and Abby were kidnapped by Hoyt, we return to my room and wait, and wait, and wait. It's been hours, and the night sky reflects my anxiety. Lightning flashes in the distance while far-off thunder grumbles threateningly.

Easton snatches the phone from the bedside table but sighs and shakes his head, showing me the screen. 'Mom' and a phone number flash there. We've been anticipating a call from Hoyt, like he did when he took Aunt Charlotte from our home on prom night. I jump up from the bed where we've been sitting, open the door, and walk out into the parking lot to stare up at the cloud-filled sky. I've never really believed in wishing on a star, but I would wish on a million right now if I could only see them.

I hear Easton reassuring his mother that they're having a great time, and he's fine. While I understand that's probably the best thing for his mother's peace of mind, I still feel bad that he's lying to her, a woman I don't know but to whom I owe so much. After all, she raised this amazing boy who's become so important to me. And realizing that I've never met, and probably never will, heightens the sadness.

"Love you, too, Mom. Bye." Easton's phone beeps as he breaks the connection and joins me outside. He puts his arm around me and snugs me into his side.

"You should sleep," I say as he turns us both around and steps inside.

"We both should sleep." He yawns.

"You stayed up with me last night, remember? I'll stay up and listen for the phone." It seems impossible that just last night everything was normal—well, maybe not normal but definitely not as screwed up as it is now.

Yawning again so hard his eyes fill with tears, Easton plops down on the bed and takes off his shoes. "Vivian, I don't think either of us would sleep through the phone ringing. I'll make you a deal. I'll sleep if you will." He pulls his t-shirt over his head, and for a moment, I can only stare. I'd forgotten (crazy, I know) how unbelievably hot Easton is. Guess I've been slightly distracted by the crazy guy kidnapping and killing people close to me. But for now, I am completely focused on this half-naked Adonis who is standing three feet away pulling the belt from his khaki shorts.

"Easton! What are you doing?" I cover my eyes like a six year old who's just seen her parents making out.

He laughs. "Relax, babe. I'm just getting more comfortable." I hear the noisy bed springs creak slightly, and I peak through my fingers. "You can uncover your eyes."

He has the cover modestly pulled up to his chin, but the grin he's giving me is most definitely not innocent.

"We're gonna *sleep*. You're idea, remember?" He throws my own suggestion back at me. I cross to the dresser and remove my least ratty pajamas. "I hope you can control yourself," he says in mock distress, "and not attack me."

Rolling my eyes, I head toward the bathroom. He chuckles, very amused at my expense. Before I close the door, he pushes a thought into my head.

At least not right away.

"Very funny," I say and close the door on his suggestive laugh.

* * *

Despite Easton's reassurance, I fight the drowsiness that threatens to overtake me. I've been lying here for at least an hour. I don't want to take a chance I'll miss Hoyt's call, but the room's darkness and Easton's steady breathing beside me lull me until my body relaxes into the curve of his arm.

My eyes flash open, and I jerk upright, panting. I'm in my bed, not the bed at the Shady Rest but my bed in the house I shared with Aunt Charlotte. A cool breeze from the open window flutters the curtain and rustles the papers on my desk. The bright moonlight fills the room with soft light, and I see that everything is just as I left it. My shimmery prom dress lies in a ruined puddle on the floor; my closet door stands open where Easton searched the floor for the nonexistent map I sent him to find so that I could lock him inside of here. Everything is the same except Easton lies beside me.

"Easton"—I touch his shoulder—"Easton, wake up."

His eyes fly open, and he jolts to a sitting position. "Did the phone ring?" He looks to his left, searching for his cell on the bedside table. That's when he realizes where he is. "What the hell?" He looks around in confusion. "Vivian, this is your room."

"Yeah, I see that."

"But how? It's gotta be a dream, right?" He rubs the sheet with his hand then touches my arm as if to see if we're both real.

"The same dream? We're both having the same dream? No, it's a trick. He's playing mind games with us." I toss back the covers and slip out of bed. Easton follows, sliding across the bed to stand next to me.

Easton walks to the lamp on my desk and tries to turn it on. It doesn't work because I broke that lamp the night I showed Easton my powers. Unsurprised, he walks to the door, the one I modified to keep him locked inside while I escaped in Aunt Charlotte's car. He touches the melted hinges and the splintered frame where I assume Cooper broke it down to get him out. "Pretty vivid dream, babe. The lamp, the door"—he walks to my prom dress and picks it up, letting the silky material slide through his fingers—"your dress—it's all exactly right."

Then I feel it, the tingle, the tug against me, willing me outside. "He's here, outside. I sense him." Not surprising considering this whole dream sequence is his creation. I grab Easton's hand. He gives me a reassuring squeeze, and we head downstairs through the kitchen, the living room, and the front door. On the porch, we stop.

Standing in the center of the front yard is my nemesis, Hoyt Matthews. He is exactly as I remember him, abnormally tall, black militant uniform, the scar I unknowingly gave him across his left eyebrow, and eyes like shiny black marbles, strangely reflecting the moon's glow. The last time I saw him he tried to kill me because I refused to join his organization.

"Ah, my dear, reunited at last!" His smooth, melodic voice and cajoling smile contradicts his bloodthirsty nature like a hypnotic cobra. "And you've brought the boy! Wonderful, just wonderful!" When I step farther out onto the porch and closer to him, his eyes narrow, and I wonder if he's remembering our last encounter when I hurled a flaming van at him.

"Do you approve of our setting?" His smile returns as he gestures around with a flip of his fingers.

"Where are Abby and Copper?" I ask, ready to have it out and get this over with. Being this close to him brings back that night last spring, and that brings back Aunt Charlotte's death, *and that* pisses me off. I'm trying to stay calm, knowing he wins if I lose my temper, my control. This very dream shows the potency of his power. He can manipulate the mind so easily that he can create a dream experienced by two people and real enough that I can feel every nick in the wooden porch beneath my feet and smell the honeysuckle from what remains of Aunt Charlotte's garden.

"Patience, my dear. All in good time. Speaking of time"—he meanders to a nearby rosebush and plucks a perfect, red bud, which he holds to his nose like a bad engagement ring commercial—"Our little reunion was bound to happen. We are too connected not to end up together. In fact, I'm a bit surprised it's taken this long." As he begins to pluck the petals from the rose, he closes the distance to the porch and motions toward Easton with what remains of the rose. "I owe your boyfriend a small morsel of gratitude. He's part of the reason I've been able to communicate with you."

"Communicate? Is that what you call your sick visions? You murdered Mr. Lewis!" I throw my hand into the air, but Easton snakes his arm around my waist and jerks me back into the porch's shadows.

Hoyt's eyes widen then he chuckles. "Temper, temper, Vivian."

But he's too late to cover his initial reaction. In that quick widening of his obsidian eyes, I saw hesitation, and I realize he's afraid. He's scared of my ability.

"Very wise, Easton. But you always could calm her. Could you not, boy?" He raises his brows, and Easton and I share a look. How could he possibly know that? He smirks.

"Oh yes, I know a great deal, my dear. You see, I used Easton's uncanny connection to you as"—he pauses, searching for the word, then smiles, teeth flashing when he finds it—"a conductor of sorts. I can't get into your head. You are too strong for that, but his mind, well, that was easy." He turns and saunters back out into the yard where he pulls a knife from a holster attached to his thigh.

"It's an unusual occurrence, this link you two have." He shrugs. "But with your history"—he chuckles humorlessly at his cleverness—"he was bound to find you. Lewis just made it that much easier. Stupid old fool! He shouldn't have refused me, but in the end, I got you all after all!" He tosses the knife into the air and catches it by the handle without looking.

A million thoughts stampede through my head. Easton and I have a history? Up until five months ago, we didn't even know each other. I know we have something special, but how would he know anything about it, about us. Does he know we can sense each other? I decide to go for the easier question, though.

"What did Mr. Lewis have to do with any of this?"

"Vivian, I gave you more credit than that! I thought you would have figured that out for yourself. Didn't that aunt of yours teach you to reason? But you'll figure it all out sooner or later." At the mention of Aunt Charlotte, my temper overrides my reason and Easton's presence. Light bursts behind my eyelids, and energy explodes from my hand.

Hoyt's taken by surprise, the blast knocking him off his feet and into the air. He lands with a thud and skids backward on his back.

"Vivian!" Easton yells and jerks my hand down again. "This is his party. He's controlling all of this!" He gestures around with his free hand. "Don't let him draw you into a fight, not here!" Before I can even take a deep breath, an invisible gust throws both of us back, pinning us to the wall of the house, our feet no longer touching the porch.

Hoyt is standing close to the porch with both of his hands raised and his palms facing us. I can't move, and for a second, I can't even breathe.

"That was foolish, my dear. You should listen to the boy. You can't win here."

Struggling against the force, I say, "Maybe not here, but back in reality, you aren't as sure, are you?" When he only continues staring with those soulless eyes, I have my answer. I might not be able to fight him in this dream world, but I will get the satisfaction of seeing his fear. "That's why you haven't come for me directly. You know you can't win. You took Aunt Charlotte, Mr. Lewis, Abby, and Cooper because you can't come for me."

He drops his hands, and we slide down the wall to land hard on our butts. "Vivian, it's all about motivation. I have no doubt that you'll come around to my way of thinking eventually. You *will* join with me and my colleagues, but until then, you just need a little push."

"I will *never* help you!" I get to my feet.

"Oh, I think you will." He raises one hand, and Easton rockets back up the wall, knocking down the hanging planter Aunt Charlotte always kept there. The surge of hot air swirls my hair into my face.

"Stop! Stop it!" I raise my own hand, which radiates a pulsing blue light, and he releases Easton who falls hard again, landing on his side.

I rush to him and kneel. Blood smears his left shoulder and back and runs diagonally toward the porch. Pressing my hand against the puncture, I realize what made the wound—the nail that used to hold our spare key behind the planter. He grunts when I press harder to stop the bleeding.

"Motivation, Vivian. It's a very useful tool. That's your problem; you care too much. Unfortunate, really, your father was the same way," he says, shaking his head in a semblance of regret. "It's so much more pleasant if new inductees are willing, but"—he shrugs—"even if they are not, they always see reason. It just takes the proper motivation." He paces in front of the porch.

"And killing Mr. Lewis is supposed to motivate me, show me what will happen to my friends if I don't agree to work with you?" Putting Easton's arm around my neck, I support him when tries to sit up and lean back against the wall.

"Yes and no. That wasn't my only reason. Mr. Lewis and I had unfinished business. Killing him was gratifying. It did help that you had grown so fond of him, but that wasn't my reason. He was disloyal and disobedient. He deserved his ending."

"So he is dead? It wasn't some circus trick where you planted that image in my head?" As much as I want this visit to be over, I need answers.

"Oh no, Vivian. It was most definitely real. Did you enjoy it? But the fact is I didn't plant the vision in *your* head at all." He points

to Easton. "I embedded it in *his*. He just couldn't see it, but you" —
he tilts his head with a look of interest on his face—"you pulled it
right out, didn't you?" He purses his lips. "You didn't even know
you were doing it. I wasn't sure it would work, but it made for a
fascinating experiment, very enlightening." Shaking his head, he
continues, "You don't find it strange that you'd never had a vision
until he came back?" He throws back his head and laughs mania-
cally, like the villain in every scary movie I've ever seen.

"Really, my dear. You must join me if for no other reason than
to teach you a thing or two about yourself. I know more about you
than you do."

I narrow my eyes. Is this a lie, some kind of trick to make me
more interested? Then it dawns on me. He's never lied. He's been
brutal and savage, but he always does and acts the way I expect.

He lunges at the porch, grabbing the railing and leaning within a
couple of feet of us. "If you join me, I can tell you everything. I can
answer every question—where you get your power, why the two of
you are connected"—he gestures between the two of us then drops
the big one, the answer he knows I want more than anything—"who
your father is…"

I swallow, my mouth suddenly dry as the Sahara. I want those
answers more than I want to wake up from this dream, and I'm so
tempted. But that's what he wants, and I'll be damned if I make this
easy for him.

"I'll get those answers without you. Go to hell, Hoyt!"

He pulls back away from the porch; an unnerving smile spreads
across his face and gives those soulless eyes an even more sinister slant.

"Most assuredly, my dear. I'll save you and your friends a spot."

CHAPTER SIXTEEN

WITH A BRILLIANT FLASH OF LIGHT, I wake up. This time I'm in my room at the Shady Rest. Easton wakes, too. For a moment we can only stare at each other before he sits up and yanks me to him in a bone-crushing hug.

"Easton, I can't breathe," I squeak out with what little breath I have left.

"Sorry," he says, releasing me. "Was any of that real?"

As I pull away from him, he grabs my hand. "You're hurt! Look!" He shows me my palm, which is bright red with fresh blood.

"It's not mine." I gently angle his torso so that I can see the back of his shoulder. There, in all its gruesome glory, is the wound he suffered when Hoyt hoisted him onto that nail. "I think this answers your question. It was definitely real. Stay put while I find something to put on this." I jump out of bed and rush to the bathroom where I gather the few medical supplies I have and some clean towels.

"Lie down," I order him when I return and lay out the supplies on the small table. "This may sting a little." I'm lying; the alcohol is going to burn severely.

He sucks in his breath and hisses air through his teeth as I pour the liquid and wipe away the blood.

"How?" he grunts.

"How what?" I ask, trying to assess how badly he's hurt.

"How did he do that? How did he take us physically there but here at the same time?" he asks between the breath he's holding and releasing in an effort to remain still while I prod and poke the puncture and torn skin around it.

"I don't know. He's very powerful."

"Yeah, but he's scared of you. That much was obvious."

I dab the wound with some antibiotic ointment and apply two large Band-Aids. "Maybe." The look in Hoyt's eyes whenever I raised my hand was true fear, but I don't want Easton to feel encouraged by that. Hoyt's a dangerous man, and his fear will only make him more so. "But I don't know why. He teleported us or something to my home hundreds of miles away and tossed us around like trash! Easton, what am I going to do?" I cover my face with my hands.

Sitting up and turning to me, he drapes his arm around my lower back. "You mean what are *we* gonna do. I'm in this, too." He huffs out a humorless chuckle. "He's using me, Viv, to communicate with you. I'm his personal cell phone!"

"As long as he has Coop and Abby, I have no choice but to do as he says. I'm his to command. That's probably another reason he took them. He knows I won't let him kill them. I'm his puppet." I slump against him. "I'm so tired, Easton." I never asked for any of this mess, and I just want it to be over. I want my friends safe. "I have to go to him, give myself up."

Easton clutches me firmly against him. "No, we have no guarantee he won't kill them anyway if you surrender."

"He won't kill them. Until he completely brainwashes me into joining him, he knows I won't help him without 'motivation.'" I sneer the last word. "He needs me compliant, and they are his only leverage. He'll contact us again." I pull away from his embrace and stand. "He's probably listening to this entire conversation right now!"

Easton runs his hands through his midnight hair. "How can I stop that? Teach me to block him or whatever it is you do to keep him out of your head."

"That's just it. I don't know how! I don't *do* anything." My frustration is overwhelming. It drains my energy, and I'm really beginning to feel rundown, literally.

As I pace toward the door, a brilliant light blinds me, and I grab for the chair. I see Abby in a van, the kind I saw in the park last spring when I tried to rescue Aunt Charlotte, except this time a wire partition separates the back from the driver and his partner up front.

Abby is crying, her mascara smeared across her cheeks. A shackle attached to her left wrist and another to her left ankle keep her close to the side of the van. When the van stops, the driver and his partner get out. Guns drawn, they fling open the back doors, and a third man enters with a set of keys. All three men wear the same all-black, militant uniform that Hoyt wears. Unsmiling and battle-scarred, they fit the bill for his men.

"Get the girl first," one of the men says. "We'll have to get back up for the boy."

Abby only cries harder when the man with the keys frees her wrist and ankle. She rubs the ugly red abrasions caused by the restraints. Bruises have already begun to form there. He grabs her roughly by the hair.

"Come on!" he yells, and Abby struggles to slide and knee-walk across the van to the open doors. She screams when he yanks her forward and makes her fall out of the opening where she lands face-first on the chat-covered ground.

"Don't touch 'er, you bastard!" The voice seems to come from my vantage point, so I assume I am seeing all this through Coop's eyes. Coop lurches toward her, but the restraints on both of his wrists and ankles prevent him from moving far.

The man with the keys turns in Coop's direction.

"You, asshole! When I get outta these"—he jerks against the shackles again hard enough to cause a small trickle of blood down his right forearm—"I'm gonna kill you!"

The man only shakes his head and smiles. "Doubtful, kid, but I'll enjoy your attempt." Then he backhands Coop's face, which only heightens Coop's fury and causes him to make a growling-like sound deep in his chest.

A second and third man enter the small space, and while the key man releases his shackles, they try to restrain Coop. As soon as both wrists are freed, they shove him down on his stomach, yank his hands behind his back, and handcuff him. They smash his face against the floor of the van while they undo his ankle restraints. But they've underestimated his strength. Coop's a fighter when he gets riled, and messing with Abby tops the list of things that make him furious.

As soon as the man releases his ankles, Coop kicks out violently, sending the guy crashing into the wire partition. The other two men, momentarily shocked, let up just enough for Coop to struggle free of them. He slams back against the van's side and kicks both feet simultaneously into the faces of the two men, who collide into the first guy as he tries to rise. A fourth man leaps into the van, points a Taser, and shoots Coop in the chest. His scream ends my vision.

When I return to reality, I'm on my knees, and Easton's kneeling next to me. He doesn't even have to ask. He knows I've had a vision.

"It was Coop and Abby. Hoyt's men were unloading them out of a van."

"Are they okay? Could you tell if they are hurt?" His concerns knifes through me. I know I said I'd stop feeling so guilty, but seeing Abby's tears and Coop's rage makes the guilt gnaw at me like a ravenous dog.

"Abby was crying," I say, unable to meet his eye.

"And Coop?" He can tell I'm deliberately hedging this question. "Vivan, what about Coop? Is he alive?"

"Yes!" I exclaim, finally looking back at him. "He was fighting them, and he wasn't really winning." I twist my hands nervously. Will this be what pushes Easton away for good? I don't think I can do this without him now. The more time we spend together, the more connected we've become—at least the more attached I've become. But Easton doesn't look angry. He's smiling.

"Good. That's good, babe. I know Cooper. When he stops fighting, that's when we have a real problem," he says, relief in his voice and eyes.

As he's helping me up, his phone rings where it lies on the table. Rushing to it, he nearly drops it when he snatches it up and pushes the answer prompt on the screen.

"Hello." He listens for a minute then looks at the screen. When he slips the phone in his pocket, I grab his arm.

"Well? Was it Hoyt?"

Taking a deep breath, he turns toward me. "I don't think so. It was a man's voice but not his. He said that someone would be here in an hour."

I sigh. "So this is it, huh? We just wait to be loaded up?"

"No, we don't. We pack." He walks to the dresser and begins pulling out my clothes.

"Pack? You think they're gonna let us take our clothes? This isn't a vacation, Easton." I grab the t-shirts he's stacking on the bed. He snatches them back.

"I know that. We may have to go with them, but we aren't giving up. If we manage to get to Abby and Coop, then escape, we'll need stuff." He starts cramming clothes into my backpack. "You're the expert on running, right?" I can't help but notice the sarcastic lilt in his tone as he continues to shove in clothes.

Crossing my arms, I glare at him. "I'm going to ignore that." He turns, and I raise my brows and tap my foot.

Shaking his head, he pulls me to him and kisses me quickly on the lips. "Here," he says, pushing the bag into my hands, "finish, and put in some first-aid supplies, too. I'm going to pack a bag for me and Coop. When you're done, pack one for Abby." He yanks on his shirt and shoes then turns, hurrying to the door.

I huff, "You could be a little nicer about it."

Easton stops with his hand on the knob. Looking over his shoulder, he grins, "Please."

*   *   *

I dress quickly after Easton's departure then rush to Abby's room. After digging around in Abby's suitcase, I throw everything in a large tote bag I found in her SUV and head back to my room to wait for Easton. Our hour is almost up by the time he returns, a bundle of nervous energy. Two backpacks are slung over his broad shoulders, and he's carrying a bulging grocery bag.

"What took you so long?" I snap. This anticipation is starting to wear on me.

"I went to the truck stop to get some food for our packs—beef jerky, peanuts, food that won't spoil—just in case," he says, transferring some of his goodies to all of our bags.

"You really think they'll let us take these along?" I ask, agitated by his efficiency. How is he always so calm and collected?

"Yeah, I do. They want you, babe. You'll tell them we're bringing the bags, or we aren't going at all." He zips my backpack with difficulty.

"I don't think we're in a position to make demands, Easton. They have our friends."

"Don't you see how desperate they are to have you?" He removes one of his shirts so that he can rearrange his bag to hold some bottles of water. "Right now, you're an unknown quantity. They have no way of knowing exactly how you'll react. We have to use that to our advantage while we can. Keep them guessing. Be unpredictable." He grabs me and hauls me firmly against him.

"We still talkin' about me?" I ask, my heart beating faster as I drown in the lagoon of his gaze.

"We have no way of knowing how long we'll get to stay together, Vivian. Most likely we'll be separated regardless." He grips me tighter. "Protect yourself no matter what happens to me, Cooper, or Abby. Don't give me that look. I'm serious. You can't let them beat you. Keep fighting, and keep them wondering what you'll do next. Don't let them know how much you want to keep us safe. If you do, you'll lose your advantage."

I shake my head, not believing what he wants me to pretend. "Easton, that will never work! No way! Hoyt already knows how connected we are. He knows I'll do anything to protect you three; otherwise, he would not be coming to collect us."

"Yeah, he knows, but when the time comes, you have to be willing to call his bluff, Viv." He pushes a stray curl that has slipped from my messy bun behind my ear and rests his hand on my neck.

"I can't. You said yourself we have no guarantees. I—" He presses his lips to mine and silences my protests. His hands slide over my back, the heat warming my skin through the thin fabric of my shirt. I slip my arms around his neck and hold him even closer. This may be the last time we have any privacy, and I intend to take advantage of it.

CHAPTER SEVENTEEN

I BUMP MY HEAD on the van's side for what feels like the hundredth time. My butt went numb about an hour into the trip, but my feet have pins and needles from staying in a seated position for so long. I rub the spot on the back of my head, and Easton puts his arm around my back.

"Maybe we'll stop again soon," he says as he pulls me in closer and rubs my sore head.

"I hope so." We've been in the back of this van for at least three hours. I have no way of knowing for sure since they confiscated Easton's phone when they loaded us inside. He was right about the bags, though. At first the two men had tried to take them, but I 'convinced' them to let us keep them by refusing to go otherwise and giving them a few well-aimed jolts. They searched the bags then tossed them and us inside.

I was shocked when they didn't try to chain us with the wrist and ankle shackles, but one of the men, the one with a patch over his right eye, seeing the direction of my gaze, had said, "The commander said that there would be no need to restrain you two."

"And you think that's a smart choice?" My temper flared at the idea that he underestimated me.

"I'm following orders—for now," he'd replied as he stepped out and shut the doors.

One bathroom stop and several hours later, I'm still fuming at the notion he expects me to be so docile, harmless enough to trust. I think Easton had the right idea when he told me to keep Hoyt guessing.

When the driver, a fleshy wall with no neck and no hair, makes a sharp left turn and slings Easton and me into the unforgiving metal floor, I decide it's time I begin doing exactly that.

"Stop the van. We need to stretch," I demand, pushing myself off of Easton who has taken the brunt of our fall.

Neither man responds or even acts like he can hear me.

"I said we need to stop." I raise my voice, and Easton raises his brows.

"What are you doing, babe?"

"Taking your advice" I crawl closer to the front where a wire wall separates us from them.

"Hey! You two lose your hearing?" I slam the flat of my hand against the cage between the two men and curl my fingers into the wire.

Without turning to look at me, One-Eye says, "Go back and sit down. We aren't stopping for another thirty minutes."

I weigh my options. Let this jerk order me around or be like Cooper and fight back? Of course, Cooper lost, but I have something he didn't.

"Listen, Cyclops, pull over right now or you and Mr. Clean are gonna have to explain to Commander Asshole why you're stranded in the middle of nowhere with a van that won't start and no prisoners inside."

Slowly, One-Eye turns his head and looks at me, squinting his single eye. "Go back and sit down." He doesn't raise his voice, but it's clear he means business. But, so do I.

I shrug. "Um... I don't think so. Can't say I didn't warn you." A tiny blue current shoots from my hand through the openings in the wire partition and straight into the van's console. Immediately, the van's warning lights flash on as the engine dies.

"What the hell?!" the driver yells, fighting the wheel as the van pulls sharply to the right. He wrestles the van to the side of the road, momentarily sliding on the loose chat covering the shoulder, until it slams to an abrupt stop.

One-Eye whips around so quickly that he startles me, and I jump back till I remember I'm supposed to be tough. Stiffening my spine, I glare right back. "Told you so. Guess we'll be stopping now." I hope he believes this macho act.

Mr. Clean turns the key, trying to restart the van. "Nothing," he says, "it's completely dead."

"Yeah, I'd say she killed the battery." One-Eye doesn't take his eyes—eye—off of me.

Mr. Clean finally turns around to join the evil eye party. "Is that all you did? Drain the battery?"

"Maybe," I shrug again. "Let us out for a few minutes and I'll fix it." I hope I'm telling the truth. I really have no clue if I can start the van again or not. Looking at each other, the two men seem to be trying to decide what to do, so I scoot next to Easton, pretending nonchalance.

He grins. "Nice. One point for the good guys."

I'm not so sure, then I hear Mr. Clean say, "What choice do we have, Ferguson? You want to call headquarters and tell Commander Matthews we need back up because we let a teenage girl get the better of us?"

Ferguson grudgingly shakes his head. "You're right." Turning fully around, he glowers at us. "We have orders to bring you in by 2300 hours. If we don't or we haven't radioed in by then, your friends will be killed. So, if this is an attempt to escape, you might want to rethink it, sweetie pie." His lips curl in sarcasm. "And I hope for their sakes you can restart this van."

Me too, but I only scowl and cross my arms. "Understood. Now let us out."

Both men check their guns and Tasers before opening the doors and stepping out. Seconds later, they unlock the van doors.

"Out." Ferguson motions us out with his gun. "Wallis, time them. They have exactly five minutes."

Wallis nods, lifting his wrist and pushing two buttons on his watch in quick succession.

"You keep an eye on him." Ferguson motions to Easton. "Sweetie pie's all mine." His leer makes my skin crawl, but I refuse to let him know. "Separate." With a flick of the gun, he motions me around the side of the van closest to the woods. For the first time I take a good look around. The sun is down, but the moon is not yet up. Twilight's my least favorite part of the day, when time holds its breath. The day's dead, but the night's unborn. It's that in-between feeling, and it reminds me too much of my own life—more than normal but not quite extraordinary. The trees are shadowed, and it's obvious from the cooler air that we've traveled farther north, toward some mountains which I see in the distance.

"Is that where we're going?" I ask pointing at the horizon.

But Ferguson just grunts. "Five minutes. Don't go far." He hands me a flashlight, which I toss back at his face. Unfortunately, he catches it before it smacks his nose. For a guy with one eye, he has pretty quick reflexes.

"No thanks." Flipping over my hand, I form an energy orb just to watch his eyes widen in shock. I could have waited until I actually got into the woods, but this made a whole lot bigger impression on him. I let it grow until it's the size of a softball then toss it back and forth between my hands. When he's good and mesmerized, I lurch forward as though I intend to send it right into his face. He leaps back and jerks the gun up only to realize I'm still holding the orb. I smile, remembering the way he made my skin crawl earlier and feeling a tiny bit of satisfaction from his response.

His face hardens. "Three minutes," he snarls.

I turn my back to him, walk far enough into the woods to shield myself from his view, take care of my business, then return to him with a minute to spare. When we get back to the van, Easton and Wallis are waiting. The tension in Easton's face melts into relief. The timer on Wallis's watch beeps annoyingly as he opens the door for Easton to climb inside. Before I can follow, Ferguson roughly seizes my upper arm.

"Not so fast. You have a van to start. Wallis, you get behind the wheel." He yanks me around the passenger side away from view since the van has windows only in the front. I hear the door slam, and Easton yells my name.

Ferguson pushes me forcefully against the side of the van and pins my shoulder with his enormous hand while shoving his gun close to my face. "This better work, or you and I are going to have a real problem. I don't give a damn what you can do." He pulls his hand away and lifts up the eye patch where I assumed there would be an empty hole. Instead I see an eye of deep brown, reminding of a freshly-plowed field. It's what I imagine a huge vat of milk chocolate would resemble, almost beautiful except this eye has no pupil. It's completely normal but is strangely absent a dark center. As soon as he lifts the patch, the ground beneath my feet gives a tiny tremble. I barely feel it, but it's definitely there. When the van at my back begins to rock as well, he drops the patch back into place.

"See, you aren't the only one with power. I'm an Element, too, maybe not as strong as you but strong enough to ensure an unpleasant situation for you and lover boy." I can only stare stupidly at him. How did he do that? This must be how other people feel when I use my power. I'm speechless as he again yanks me forward toward the front of the van. The hood's latch pops, and Ferguson lifts it so that the engine is visible. Thunder rolls in the distance.

I have no experience with motors, and when I continue to gawk uncertainly, he grabs my right hand, tugs it toward the battery, and slaps it down on top of it, causing me to stumble into the front of the van. The sky rumbles overhead now, and I jump when he says, "Do it. Zap the battery or whatever the hell you do."

Only problem is I can't seem to do anything. I haven't had any problems using my powers, controlling them 'yes' but using them 'no', until this moment. My brain is still totally dumbfounded by what I've just seen. I guess I'd assumed only Hoyt and I have powers even though he hinted at Mr. Lewis's abilities. Till now, though, I'd only witnessed mine and his, leaving me completely unprepared to feel the ground moving just because this guy shows me his weird eye.

"What's the matter?" He shakes my wrist. "You outta juice? Aw, did I shake you up?" He smirks at his own joke. "Guess you're not as tough as you think you are, huh, sweetie pie?" That's enough to piss me off which in turn switches on my power and sends a current into the battery. The van springs to life as a raindrop plops on my nose.

"Very good," he says as though I'm a toddler. When he yanks me back from the hood, I scrape my forearm against a sharp edge of metal, causing me to grunt and jerk it to my chest.

He slams the hood and grabs that arm to pull me around the van, but as I'm attempting to twist out of his grip, he notices the tiny trail of blood beginning to ooze from the cut. Before both our eyes, the cut closes, as if I've magically glued it back together. Only the bright line of red remains less than a minute later.

Ferguson's quizzical look speaks volumes as he stands, head tilted, holding my forearm. Light rain causes the blood to spider-web across my arm. "You're a Healer, too?"

Slinging my arm away, I swipe my hand down it erasing the evidence completely. Since I have no idea how to respond to his question, I glare at him and walk in silence to the back of the van as the rain begins to patter against the ground.

"You okay?" Easton asks as I settle in beside him once again, my butt immediately protesting. Knowing we have no privacy I really can't say what I want to say aloud. Good thing I have a solution.

When Wallis pulls onto the road, I put my hands on Easton's face and show him what I've seen and heard in our short recess. I haven't even had time to process this myself. I'm an Element and a Healer, whatever that means, and a guy just created a mini earthquake on the side of the road with his eye! Easton's face is as shocked as I feel.

"What does all this mean, Easton?" I drop my hands.

"It means you have to be willing to fight back with everything you've got. If one of these guys gets in your face, you have to be willing to hurt someone, Vivian. No matter what." He leans back and tucks me into his side.

"You mean *kill* someone?" I know he's 100 percent correct, but I don't know if I'll ever be able to actually do it.

"Try to sleep. We don't know what it'll be like where we're going." He closes his eyes and sighs deeply. For a minute, I stare at his face then I snug into his shoulder and take his advice.

CHAPTER EIGHTEEN

WHEN THE VAN DOORS OPEN, fear overwhelms me. The darkness is so thick that I swear I feel it press against my face. The cool air raises goose bumps along my arms. Every unnerving movement echoes into a pitch-black distance.

Ferguson waves us out with a fluorescent glow stick like kids use at Halloween. When I step down, the stone beneath me is slightly damp and slippery. Had Easton not been helping me down, I'd have fallen for sure. As soon as I feel Easton beside me, I create a light orb, hold it high and look around.

We are surrounded by rock, the ceiling, the floor, the walls—everything. Moisture creeps along the walls, sometimes dripping from the ceiling and adding to our own footstep echoes. Sharp curves lie both behind and ahead of us, but the space is wide enough and tall enough to allow the van, and probably larger vehicles, through easily.

"A cave? We're in a cave?" I ask as Ferguson lifts his wrist and speaks into a small device.

"Retrieval team clear." He then presses against his ear where I notice for the first time a small, hearing-aid like device glint in the light of my orb. "Roger," he replies into his wrist and nods to Wallis.

Positioning himself in the lead, Wallis walks toward the cave wall. Ferguson steps behind us. "Move," he says forcefully as he draws his gun.

Easton takes my hand, and we follow Wallis. As we near the cave wall I notice the moisture on the wall is heavier, less of a creeping and more like running. It pools a little along the base of the cave and drips more rapidly from the ceiling, plopping on our heads almost like a light rain and reminding me of how thin my shirt is where it clings cold and wet to my shoulders.

"Damn!" Ferguson exclaims, wiping water from his eye.

"It's her again," Wallis says, tossing the words over his shoulder in Ferguson's direction.

"I know," he snaps.

Easton and I exchange looks as I enter his mind.

Her? Her who? And what's she doing?

He shrugs as Ferguson pushes closer to us. The space around us narrows as we squeeze between a rock crevice barely wide enough to allow the men to walk through facing forward. The claustrophobic hollow ends abruptly, and Wallis stands in front of a rock wall. He nods up at the rock ceiling, and the wall before us begins to slide slowly almost noiselessly to the right into a hidden panel made to resemble solid rock. We step into a metal-lined room. The top, bottom, and sides are some kind of shiny metal which reflects our images in a funhouse affect and makes my head feel strange. As soon as Ferguson steps in, the wall slides closed behind him. Wallis presses his hand against a glass-like surface where a bright, orange light scans it.

Dizziness begins to make my stomach twist, and in the short time it takes for another sliding door to open, I feel faint, uncertain I'll even be able to walk through the opening on my own. Easton must be feeling the effects, too, because he sways beside me and releases my hand to grab for the wall, but the slick surface offers no support, and he crumples to the reflective floor.

Ferguson holsters his gun and puts his arms under Easton, pulling him up enough to drag him through the opening. My knees give, but before I hit the floor Wallis scoops me up and walks through.

"What... why did...?"

"It's designed to create a feeling of sickness in order to weaken anyone, even people like you." He carries me to one of several couches in this new room.

"Why aren't you sick?" My stomach lurches, and I'm pretty sure I'm going to hurl any minute.

"Training." He opens a drawer on a small table next to the couch, pulling out a white baggy, and handing it to me. "Don't puke on the floor, okay?" He almost smiles as he pats my knee. "I did the first, oh I don't know, twelve times." When he finally allows himself to smile, he looks a whole lot friendlier. "It'll pass in a few minutes."

As he moves away, I glance around the room which is a complete whiteout. The walls, couches, and tables are pristine as new snow. It isn't large and it isn't like home, but it's much more welcoming than the room-o-barf.

After Ferguson deposits a groaning Easton on a couch across from me, he checks his watch. "Thirty minutes to spare," he says with smug satisfaction, "even with her little field trip." He jerks his thumb in my direction and slaps Wallis on the back as though they've won a championship basketball game instead of kidnapping two teenagers. He pulls a black bottle from one of his pockets, opens it, and holds it under Easton's nose. He shakes Easton and stoops close to his face, shouting, "Hey, wake up!"

Easton's eyes eventually flutter open in confusion at first. Then his face pales beneath that tan complexion. "Think I'm gonna—" He leans between his knees and throws up. Ferguson isn't quite quick enough to avoid the eruption and vomit splatters his legs and covers his shoes, making me indescribably happy.

"Shit!" He jumps and looks down at the runny mess.

Easton leans back, covering his face with his hands and moaning. Ferguson steps furiously toward him. My weakness vanishes as I throw up my hand and project an energy shield around Easton where it shimmers white and blue.

Ferguson whips around in my direction. I know I shouldn't antagonize him, but I can't help myself. I never could stand a bully.

Smiling, I shrug my shoulders. "You know what they say about karma."

Even from where he stands across the room, I can see Ferguson's jaw clench as he grits his teeth. When he lifts his eye patch, Wallis steps between us, grabbing Ferguson's wrist.

"Enough," he says quietly but with authority. "Our part is finished, and you can't let her goad you into something you probably can't finish. She's a Healer and an Element with at least two properties! You can't begin to match that, and a room twenty feet in the side of a mountain is definitely not the place to use your property.

I'm *not* looking to get crushed and buried tonight." He lowers Ferguson's arm, and Ferguson shifts his gaze back to me, promising revenge in his poisonous stare.

He rolls his shoulders and pops his neck. Meanwhile, I pull the shield back into myself, feeling that familiar shock when it enters my chest.

"You get him." Wallis points to Easton who has semi-recovered. "Let's go." Wallis approaches me calmly but cautiously like he doesn't know if Ferguson and I will suddenly decide to duke it out anyway.

"Up!" Ferguson bunches his fist in the front of Easton's shirt and begins to jerk him up, but Easton jumps up and pushes Ferguson who stumbles back a step then reaches for his gun, his eyes blazing.

"Ferguson, no!" Wallis yells.

Ferguson's chest is heaving with anger as he steps back into Easton's face. Not quite as tall but a few inches broader, Ferguson is not an opponent to be taken lightly. "Tough guy now that your girlfriend is protecting you!" He stands toe-to-toe with Easton.

But Easton doesn't back down. "I don't need her help to kick your ass!"

Wallis steps in again, this time by pushing a series of numbers into a keypad beside the elevator-style doors. "Wallis, operation number seven one two," he says into a speaker beneath the number pad while a device scans his eye with a green light.

When the doors slide apart, we step through into a cavernous room with walls made of the natural rock. Computer screens flash, and more men in black uniforms look up as we enter. The doors whisper closed again after all four of us are inside.

"Lewis!" Ferguson's voice booms at my back, and a man not much older than me approaches us. "You and Wallis take this boy to the prison quarters and lock him with the others." As Lewis takes Easton's upper arm, Easton resists and jerks out of his hold.

"I'm staying with Vivian!"

Lewis and Wallis quickly slam Easton face-first against the doors behind us, yank his arms behind his back, and wrap plastic restraints on his wrists as he struggles against them. Lewis grabs a handful of his hair and smacks his face hard against the metal.

"Stop! No!" I yell, but when I try to surge out a burst of energy, nothing happens.

Ferguson laughs and grasps me around the waist from behind, pulling me back. I come up hard against his chest, kicking and flailing, but he's too strong and too tall. My feet dangle for a second as he spins me around to face him.

"It won't work here. See, Commander Matthews is too smart for that." He tweets my nose with his finger like a mischievous child. "There is a special device that scrambles our abilities." He motions around with his hand. "In most of this facility, you're on your own, as close to normal as you'll ever be." He shrugs and smirks then whips me back around against his chest. "Take him away."

Lewis yanks Easton from the wall. For a moment, our eyes meet. I try to send a message into his mind, but I can't. And for the first time ever, the thought of normalcy scares me.

"Don't worry, kid," Ferguson says, very close to my ear, "I'll take good care of her." He runs the backs of his fingers down my cheek, and my stomach twists.

"You bastard!" Easton fights again, but this time Lewis pulls a syringe from a small pocket in his uniform and injects Easton in the neck. Despite his efforts, his brow creases, and he drops to his knees. When he looks up at me again, he blinks rapid-fire while his eyes lose focus and slide shut.

"You brought it on yourself, man." Lewis motions over two more men. The four men hoist him up and carry him from the room where they disappear into a tunnel cut from the natural rock. I swallow back the tears brimming in my eyes as Ferguson laughs behind me.

"Cheer up, sweetie pie. You and I will be spending a lot of time together."

CHAPTER NINETEEN

"I'M NOT GOING TO HANDCUFF YOU because you aren't going to give me any trouble, right?" Ferguson says stepping in front of me. Every eye in this enormous room is focused on me. Easton's earlier advice rings in my head like the Liberty Bell. Even though he told me to be unpredictable, I'm not entirely sure I should now that I have no power to back it up.

Before I can reply, Ferguson grabs my arm and hauls me along beside him in the same direction Lewis, Wallis, and the other guys took Easton. The memory of Easton falling to his knees jars me, and I yank my arm from his hold, planting my feet. We may be at his mercy, but I refuse to let him know how scared I am. Inches from my face, he glares.

"You really that stupid? You really think you want to do this now that all you have to fight with is the strength in this puny body?" He pokes his finger into my chest with enough force that I have to take a step back. Maybe this isn't such a great idea after all. A voice behind me saves me from answering.

"Sir, where should we take these?" Two men approach us with the bags Easton insisted we pack.

"Take them to the prisoners. We've already searched them."

"Wait!" I exclaim before the men move away. I take my backpack from one of the men. With a nod of his head, Ferguson motions them away.

"Now, are you finished with your tantrum?" Ferguson asks, impatience clearly written in the tension around his mouth.

I glance down at the ratty bag that has long since faded from red to pink and is frayed around the edges. This bag represents all the crap I've been through since spring when this entire ordeal began. Seeing it crammed to bursting with the clothes and supplies that may have to save my life if I manage to escape creates a spark inside of me. When I remember Aunt Charlotte and my mom, the spark becomes a tingle, and faster than a snap, I'm shaking with rage. I close my eyes, see the familiar starburst explode, and feel the burn in my palm.

"Answer me!" Ferguson yells.

I open my eyes and see his shocked expression through a tunnel of white and gray.

"How the hell?" He reaches for his gun but never makes it. A blast of blue rockets him into the stone wall at his back.

Men run at me from all sides, and it's like a giant pinball machine, each man a glowing blue bull's-eye like that night at the park. I fire blast after blast that ricochet from the rock walls, and the whole place shakes with each hit. It feels amazing! The weakness and help-lessness are gone. Men are screaming, shouting orders, and running in panic until I hear the voice that haunts my nightmares.

When I swing around, Hoyt is not ten feet behind me, hold-ing Abby at gunpoint. Her eyes are huge, but I don't know if it's because she has a gun pressed to her temple or because I'm blowing up everything in sight.

"Vivian, this isn't the way to begin your training." Hoyt's voice is calm, but it doesn't hide the rigidity in his stance. My hands shake; my breathing's rapid as he steps closer. I focus on Abby's face as tears trail down her cheeks. I have to calm down, or I have no doubt he'll kill her. Closing my eyes and breathing deeply, I finally gain control, and when I open my eyes, he pushes her into my arms. We cling to each other while she sobs.

"I'm sorry, Abby. I never wanted you involved in any of this." I squeeze her to me.

"Ah! How touching! You see, my dear, motivation is key." He motions to the men standing, guns drawn, at his back. "Take her back to her quarters and wait there until you hear from me."

"No, no, Abby!" I yell as they pull her from my arms and force her from me.

"Hands, Vivian." Hoyt pulls out metal handcuffs. When I hold out both hands, he clicks on the cuffs then takes straps of a metal-like mesh and binds my hands together, palms touching. He wraps the straps over and over until my circulation is in danger.

"Carter!" He yells, and a man much smaller and less muscular than all the others appears carrying a thick rubber bag. The man, Carter, holds the bag open.

"Inside," he says in a nasally voice reminiscent of Manly Jenkins, the wimpy nerd from my English class. When I stick my hands inside, the weight of it makes me stagger forward a step. "It's rubber, lined with a special substance that hampers conductivity. My own invention." But his self-satisfactory smirk fades when he looks in Hoyt's direction.

"As was the equalizer, I believe," Hoyt replies, causing the petite man to blanch white.

"Yes, uh, well, yes, Commander. And it has worked well till now, sir."

"I believe I ordered you to install a second device before Vivian's arrival. Did I not, Carter?"

"Yes, you did, sir, but I thought that if I increased the power on the original that—"

"That was not my order, Carter!" Hoyt fists the front of the man's uniform and lifts him slightly, forcing Carter to his tiptoes. "You have not seen her abilities. I and the ten men she killed last time have!" A gust, like an invisible hand, flings Carter into a panel of monitors showing the cave's entrance.

"If it cannot control my abilities, it stands to reason it would definitely not control hers!" He walks over to Carter who groans as Hoyt kneels beside him. "She's a Double-Element." His voice is calm again, almost gentle. "Carter, install it within the hour."

Near the wall, Ferguson struggles to a sitting position, holding his badly burned arm. "She's a Healer, too, sir," he says, his voice strained as though he is in pain.

"I suspected as much, Ferguson." Hoyt doesn't look in Ferguson's direction when he replies but instead walks toward me and touches my cheek. "We will be great together, my dear. But first, I fear you will need to be broken." He slaps me hard enough to knock me to the ground. I'm momentarily rattled as I feel a trickle of blood drip from my nose onto my cheek.

I try to lift my hands to swipe it away, but the weight of the bag and the bindings is too great. He hauls me to my feet where I lock onto his obsidian gaze.

"This is your first lesson, my dear. Take her to her room." He turns to the men still awaiting orders behind him and walks briskly ahead of us but stops before going into the tunnel. Without turning, he announces loudly, "Oh, and help Ferguson to my chambers. His treatment of my guests is reprehensible, and I find he is in need of a reminder of who is in charge."

CHAPTER TWENTY

AS IF IN ANSWER TO HIS COMMAND, thunder shook the room. He ran to the still-open door to close it against the rain lashing into the workroom, but before he could reach it, Lord St. Clair, drenched and angry, appeared in the opening. Together, the two men pushed against the wind and slid the latch closed. Turning to the work table, St. Clair shouted, "She cannot be here! Remove her at once!"

Ethan stepped in front of St. Clair, blocking his view of Virginia's writhing form. "She will *not* be moved. On the morrow, you may discharge me and throw us both into the wilderness, but tonight, you will not give me orders! She stays. The babe is coming quickly!"

St. Clair's face reddened in outrage. "How dare you order me about in my own home! I'll see you in shackles, boy!"

"On the morrow, but not tonight!" Ethan clenched his fists at his sides. He did not wish to strike the older, smaller man, but he would do as he must to keep Virginia and her babe safe. Virginia's scream drew the attention of both men. Ethan, forgetting St. Clair for the moment, rushed back to her.

Tears mixed with the sweat and rain on Virginia's face as she squeezed Ethan's hand with all her might. Curled on her side with her knees drawn tightly to her chest, she knotted the fabric of the coat in her fist. Pain glazed her eyes, and she shook feverishly.

"Virginia, I don't know what to do!" Ethan shouted helplessly. "Lord St. Clair, I beg of you. Please help her if you have the knowledge," he pleaded. "She needs help, else she'll die."

When St. Clair made no move but only stared at the girl thrashing before him, Ethan grasped his shirt front and pulled him nearly across the metal table. "The babe is innocent! Do you want to meet God with the death of a child on your soul because I swear if you stand idly by and let them die, you'll not be far behind them!"

The storm's fury could not drown the agonized scream torn from Virginia's throat, and St. Clair jumped in response.

"I... I know little about female medicine," he stammered, reaching out to press his hand to Virginia's abdomen.

"Please, my lord, anything!" Ethan beseeched. "Tell me what to do!" After pausing only a moment longer, St. Clair jumped into action.

"Build the fire, boy, and turn up the lamps. I will do what I can."

Ethan rushed to the meager fire while St. Clair retrieved linens from a cupboard along the wall.

"Goody Crowe stored these old sheets for my experiments. They are worn, but they are clean. Get the kettle of water from the hook and that empty bucket," he said pointing to a small wooden bucket on a stool nearby. "There's lye soap on the mantel. Fetch it as well." He pulled away the coat Ethan had used to cover Virginia. A gasped exclamation from St. Clair made Ethan spin around quickly, bucket and kettle in hand.

Blood soaked Virginia's once-white nightshift and smeared the silver metal of the table.

CHAPTER TWENTY-ONE

"**I'VE BEEN SITTING IN THIS ROOM FOR HOURS.** Please take them off so I can use the bathroom," I whine at the door. Wallis has been posted out there for nearly the entire time. He replaced the first guard not long after I was brought here. When he arrived he opened the door to tell me that Easton, Abby, and Cooper are fine, and in a weird way, his presence is comforting—better the devil I know than the one I don't, I guess.

The room is surprisingly comfortable. It actually looks like a hotel room, a nice hotel room with a queen-size bed complete with a brown and gold comforter, soft rugs on a hardwood floor, and bedside lamps. There are no windows, presumably since we're inside of a mountain, and one wall is the natural stone, but the others are normal, painted a mellow ecru.

There is, however, a bathroom with a sink, shower, and toilet, which I am in desperate need of right now. It stands in its perfect, porcelain whiteness, taunting me because there is no way I can use it with all of this stuff over my hands.

"Pleeeeeeeeease, Wallis. I'm going to explode and flood the whole place," I beg again, shifting around doing the pee-pee dance. "I'll be good, and you can put them right back on. In fact, just take the bag off! I can do this with the rest still on." I think, I can anyway. "Besides, that Carter guy beefed up the whatever gadget thingy to keep me under control, right?" When I still get no response, I pull out the big guns.

"Well, if you're not going to let me use the toilet then I guess you'll clean up the mess because I have to go one way or another!" I *really* hope it won't come to that, but...

Before I have to embarrass myself and lose my last thread of dignity, I hear a heavy sigh, a series of musical beeps, then a click. Wallis, looking none too happy to see me, steps inside. I smile innocently, but he's not impressed.

"The bag, and that's all. You'll just have to make do with that," he grumbles as he removes the outside restraints.

When he slips the heavy bag off, it's my turn to sigh, but in relief, not agitation. "OMG! You have no idea how happy I am that you did that!"

"Just go," he says gruffly, "but leave the door open."

"You're going to watch me go?" I can't hide my shock and disbelief. When he moves the bag toward me as though he intends to slip it back on, I practically run to the bathroom.

"Okay, okay," I toss over my shoulder, turning on the bathroom light. As I'm awkwardly unbuttoning my pants, he turns his back but remains in the doorway. Normally, I'm not sure I could go with a ginormous bald buy standing a few feet away, but this isn't exactly normal. After I finish and sort of wash my hands, I hurry to his side so that he knows I'm not up to something. Wallis has been the only person to show me any kindness, and I don't want to ruin that. He might prove to be a useful ally.

"Thank you." I extend my hands to accept the torturous bag and binding again.

"You're welcome," he mumbles awkwardly as though those aren't words in his everyday vocabulary. Looking from the bag to my hands and back again, he says, "I wish I didn't have to do this."

"I know. You have orders." I finish for him, nodding. After what Hoyt just told Ferguson, I would hate to see Wallis disobey and be punished. I would feel terrible if he did. Ferguson... not so much. Ferguson's a dick. He deserves whatever he gets.

He sighs deeply and lifts his radio wrist to his mouth. "Lewis," he pauses and pushes the device in his ear, "bring One her meal."

"One, huh?" I raise my eyebrows. "I have a name."

"Not now you don't, not until you earn it. For now, you're One." He shrugs lightly as though taking away my identity is a commonplace occurrence. Maybe here it is.

"If I'm One, that means there are others." He removes the rest of my bindings.

"Well, yes. There are your friends, of course." He searches his pockets.

"So they're Two, Three, and Four?"

He produces a tiny key and unlocks the cuffs. I rub my wrists which are red and chafed a little.

"Yes, at the moment," he says, dropping the bindings, bag, and cuffs on a small table near the door.

" 'At the moment?' " Then there are or have been others.

Before he can respond, a knock sounds at the door. He draws his gun and points it at me.

Lewis's disembodied voice comes through the door. "Sir, it's Lewis. I have her food."

"Enter." Wallis keeps his gun on me. Lewis, a skinny kid barely past the acne stage, carries a tray with two covered dishes and an apple juice box. "Set it there, Lewis, and return to your post." Wallis's voice is quiet but commanding, and Lewis nods once nervously at me then leaves again.

Investigating the tray, I pull away the covers to reveal what appear to be a ham and cheese sandwich, some plain potato chips, and uncooked, baby carrots. Beneath the second, smaller cover, orange jello jiggles merrily.

"Wow, dinner always this great?" I ask drily.

"It's late. We have a full kitchen staff but not at this time of night. Tomorrow, you'll have a real meal if you behave." He carries the tray to a short ottoman in front of an oversized, brown armchair. My stomach rumbles loudly, and I nearly trip over my own feet to get to the chair. Before I realize it, I've eaten everything but the jello.

From his spot by the door, Wallis disguises his smile behind a fake cough. "Hungry?"

"Guess so," I reply around my last bite of carrot. I eye the jello. "Want this?" I curl my nose and offer the plate to Wallis.

"Don't like jello?" He doesn't try to hide his amusement as he approaches to take the tray.

I make a face. "Food shouldn't wiggle."

With a short laugh, he takes the tray, covers the plates, and speaks to his wrist again. "Lewis, retrieve the tray," he says, putting it outside the door and approaching with my hand prison again.

"Can I at least wash and brush first?"

His lips twist as his brows furrow. "You have five minutes." He sets the timer on his watch like he did earlier outside the van.

Grabbing my backpack, I mentally thank Easton for forcing me to bring it and hurry to the bathroom. Wallis stands again with his back turned as I get ready for bed. After I change into a clean shirt and a pair of sweats, wash my face, and brush my teeth, I rush to him just as a beep announces my time is up.

Throwing my bag beside the bed, I stand, hands out, in front of this bad guy who's turning out not to be so bad. He replaces the handcuffs and only lightly wraps the bindings. The bag and outside bindings he lays on the table by the door.

"Don't make me regret this, Vivian," he says looking into my eyes.

"I won't, Wallis. I promise, and thanks for being so nice to me. I figure you aren't too thrilled about being stuck with me tonight."

"Not just tonight. Lewis and I are assigned permanently to you, but I've had worse assignments." He winks at me and turns to leave.

I'm climbing into bed when he pauses before closing the door. Without looking back, he says, "And I totally agree about the jello."

The lock outside the door beeps as Wallis sets it for the night, and I wonder if he has to sleep out there. When I click off the lamp beside the bed, Easton's face flashes in my mind. I hope he's comfortable, and I make up my mind to find out for sure tomorrow.

As my eyes close, I hear his voice in my head, faint but not my imagination.

I love you, Vivian.

And I reply, hoping our love will get us through this.

CHAPTER TWENTY-TWO

A LOUD KNOCK WAKES ME from a great dream the next morning. In my dream, Easton and I were picnicking beside the lake back home while Cooper and Abby fished nearby. Abby was squealing because Cooper was shoving his latest catch in her face. We were all laughing. It was such an amazing dream that I feel like crying when the loud knocking continues.

"What!" I yell, sitting up and rubbing my eyes. The musical beeping of the number pad lock is all the warning I have before the door swings open, and Lewis enters the room.

"Prisoner One, you have been commanded to the mess hall." Lewis is wearing the black uniform that all the men here usually wear, but on him, it looks wrong. He's so skinny that the uniform hangs baggy and limp. His dark blond hair spikes around his head, stiff with gel. He can't be more than twenty or twenty-one years old.

"I have a name, and if you want me to respond you're going to have to use it." I toss the covers back and throw my legs over the edge.

Lewis clears his throat. "You have fifteen minutes to shower and dress."

When he makes no move to leave, I stand, arms akimbo, and glare at him. "What's the deal with you guys? What do you think I'm going to do? Where could I possibly go? I'm in a freakin' cave!" When he still doesn't leave, I grab my bag from the floor and head to the bathroom.

"Wait," he says, and he hands me a bag that I hadn't noticed in his hand. "You're supposed to wear this." Unzipping the bag, I find a uniform exactly like the one he's wearing, and black boots. It's black, has lots of pockets, and is very SWAT team chic.

After I shower and dress, I emerge to find Lewis still camped out beside the door. "Well, do you approve? Am I one of the guys now?" I can't keep the sarcasm from my voice. In response, he opens the door.

In a poor imitation of his voice, I say, "Yes, Prisoner One. You look appropriate for today's activities which include blowing up a hospital and drowning kittens." As I step out into the hall, he glares down at me then keys the lock on my door.

Silently, we walk down the long hallway past several doors like mine. "Are there people in those rooms?"

"Some." His honest reply surprises me.

"Will I be meeting them?"

"Sometime," he answers, turning left when the corridor finally forks.

"When will I see Easton, Abby, and Cooper?" His long strides force me to take two steps to every one of his, and I'm practically jogging to keep up.

"Soon." We stop in front of a set of sliding metal doors with a key pad.

I put my hands on my hips and pant. "Can you say more than one word at a time?"

He doesn't respond this time as he keys in a number sequence, making sure to keep his back between me and the pad as he types it in. When the door slides open and he stands aside to let me pass, I see a room filled with cafeteria-style tables and bench seating. A buffet line spreads across the front of the room, and heaping pans of scrambled eggs, sausage, bacon, and toast steam happily. The sight and smell remind me that supper consisted of a cold ham sandwich. Uniformed men and a few women sit around the tables eating, and I have that familiar 'cafeterias suck' feeling when they all turn in unison to gawk at me. A freak among freaks.

His hand on my shoulder, Lewis guides me, and the doors close behind us. "Wallis said you'd be hungry." He nudges me forward toward the buffet. Keeping my eyes locked on the front, I avoid meeting the stares of the people around me as I head to the plates.

"Where're Easton, Abby, and Cooper?" I take a big helping of eggs.

"In their cells," he replies around a strip of bacon he's just shoved in his mouth.

"When can I see them?" I watch Lewis fill a plate, too.

"That's not my call." He grabs silverware and napkins and waits for me to finish. We both pour coffee in white mugs and head to an unoccupied table in front. I sit with my back to the seeking eyes around me and stare at my plate. As hungry as I am, I can't bring myself to eat until I know I'll be seeing the others soon.

"I want to see them, Lewis," I say looking up at him.

"Well, I can't guarantee that you will." He's shoveling in eggs like a backhoe.

"It's important. Please, Lewis, just one minute." I must sound pathetic because he stops eating and looks at me.

"I can't, not until I receive the orders, One." Agitated, he moves on to attack his bacon.

"Yes, you can. Make it happen, Lewis." I'm beginning to feel agitated myself. "I've been hauled to the middle of nowhere, hidden in the side of a mountain, and forced to wear this uniform. I have no idea what I will be commanded to do next, and I want to see my friends."

A tingle starts in my chest. The tingle trills down my arm, but according to Hoyt's orders last night, Carter was supposed to install a second equalizer to neutralize my abilities. Despite that, the tingle is unquestionably there, and my palm is starting to glow lightly. It's not brilliant and bright like before, but I clench my fist to prevent Lewis from seeing the dull light. If he didn't install it yet, this might work.

Lewis raises his eyes to mine. He opens his still-full mouth to respond, but stops. His stare turns blank; his mouth drops open.

"Lewis? You okay?" I wave my hand in front of his face, but the blank stare remains as though he's in a trance. Maybe... I take a chance and close my eyes. Instantly, I'm inside his mind, probably the most organized one I've seen. Normally, I would feel guilty about messing with someone's thoughts or memories but not this time. Lewis likes orders. Okay, I'll give him some new ones.

Take me to see my friends. NOW!

I mentally pull away, and just like every hokey hypnotist act I've ever seen on television, I snap my fingers close to his face. He closes his mouth, confusion in his eyes, and looks around at the other tables.

"Good, huh?" I take a bite of my eggs as if I haven't just infiltrated his brain.

He tilts his head then shakes it and, still chewing, takes up his tray. "Come on. We need to get moving if I'm going to take you all the way across the facility." He gulps his coffee.

Standing, I grab a few strips of bacon and follow him. "Across the facility?"

He deposits his tray in a window with a conveyer that takes away the dirty dishes before taking my tray and depositing it as well. "Yes, those are my orders. Take you to see your friends then to the training center."

Jackpot!

CHAPTER TWENTY-THREE

I HAVE NO IDEA how it is possible that I was able to change Lewis's orders. Does it really matter? Hell, no! All that matters is that I'm going to see Easton, Abby, and Cooper.

The corridors become more and more twisted, and the farther into the facility we go, the colder and damper it gets. In some places the hallways are so narrow, we would have to turn sideways if we tried to pass another person. I try to memorize each turn, but I've never been the best with directions. Finally, the passageways open into one large cave with another passageway directly across from the entrance. I hear the sound of rushing water.

"Are we near a river?" I ask Lewis, who has remained quiet the entire trip.

"Yes"—he points toward the passageway across the enormous cave—"there's a river that cuts through the mountain down that corridor."

He turns to his right and begins walking toward the cave wall. Just like before, the wall isn't what it appears. A door mimics the surrounding rock. The lock is a handprint identifier tucked behind a rocklike panel. After he scans his hand, the artificial stone door slides into the wall and we step inside another hallway, more like those in the main part of the facility, but the rooms are cells complete with bars. The hallway isn't long, and we only pass one empty cell before we reach them, each housed in a different cell.

Coop is on my right; Abby is on my left across from him. Both
jump up from their twin-size cots and run to the bars. Abby reaches
out to me through the bars, and my heart sinks. Her clothes are
dirty, her face a red, swollen mess from crying. I run to her, putting
my arms through the bars to hold her.

"V! Oh, Vivian, tell me you're here to get us out!"

I pull back from her. "Not yet, Abby. But soon, I promise." I hope
I'm not lying to her. I was able to brainjack Lewis, but there's no
way we could just walk out of here. I've never tried to control more
than one person at a time, and that's what it would take to get us all
out safely. Besides, if Carter installs the second equalizer as he was
ordered, I won't be able to control *anyone*. "I need a plan first. They
aren't just going to let us go." I wipe at her face. "Please don't cry
anymore." I can't bear the sight of her pitiful face. I turn to Lewis.

"Do they have access to a shower? She needs a shower and clean
clothes. Are they being fed? When was the last time they ate?" His
expression becomes vague again as I force my way inside his mind
for a second time.

"I will radio for their assigned guards," he says turning for the
entryway. "The radio doesn't work in here." He steps out into the
main cave, and I turn back to Abby.

"They brought food yesterday, but I couldn't eat."

I give her a little shake. "You have to eat. When they bring it this
time, eat it. Whatever it is, you have to eat it. You need to be strong
if I'm going to get us out." She nods, and I turn back toward Cooper.
Where Abby is sad, Cooper is pissed!

He is standing at the bars, too. When I approach him, he pulls me
to the bars and whispers, "I'm worried about her, Vivian. It's cold in
here and I heard her shivering last night. You need to convince them
to put us together. She'll be sick if I can't help keep her warm." His
eyes are blazing but scared at the same time.

"I'll do my best, Coop."

When Lewis returns, his brow is wrinkled as though his brain is
beginning to register that something's not right. I look into his eyes
and concentrate. "Lewis, Abby should be placed with Coop."

His eyes glaze over again and he goes back out the door, holding
his wrist to his mouth as he exists.

"Are you controlling him?" Coop asks.

"I think so, but I don't know how I'm not supposed to be able to. They have a device that blocks my power, but so far ...," I shrug. "Where's Easton?" Cooper points down the hall.

One cell separates Cooper from Easton. As I approach the cell I see Easton lying still on his cot.

"Easton?" I call, but he doesn't respond. His back is toward me, his face to the rock wall. "What's wrong with him, Cooper?" Panic stretches my voice tight like a rubber band about to pop.

"I don't know. He's been like that since they brought him in here. I can't see him, but he hasn't said a thing." I close my eyes again and hold onto the bars.

Easton, talk to me.

He groans but doesn't move.

Easton, please, I can't stay long, and I need to hear your voice.

He stirs on the cot. "Vivian," he says, his voice rough from disuse.

"Yes, Easton! I'm here!" I squeeze hard on the bars, the metal heating beneath my hand. Lewis reemerges from the doorway with two other guards. He unlocks Abby's cell door with the keypad and one of the guards enters her cell while Lewis moves to Coop's door. The other guard readies his Taser.

"Lewis, are you sure this was an order? No one informed us of this move," says the guard holding Abby's arm.

"Yes, just do it," Lewis holds the door while Abby walks into Coop's arms. He immediately pulls her to the cot and covers her with his blanket. The guards moveAbby's cot and her bag.

Easton sits up and faces me, holding his head as though he's in pain. "My head," he moans. "What did they give me?"

"I don't know, but it sounds like you've been out since the injection when they first took you away."

Slowly and unsteadily, he stands and walks toward me. He puts both hands over mine on the bars. "You okay?" he whispers. His chin and cheeks are shaded in dark stubble, his eyes ringed beneath.

"Yes" — I lean in as close as possible — "I can still use my powers. I'm not supposed to be able to use them, but somehow, I can. I don't know how long it'll last, but I'm going to do everything I can to get us all out of this."

He reaches through the bars and touches my cheek, the warmth and strength of his hand seeping into me. "Be careful, Vivian.

Remember Mr. Lewis. You can't play around with these people too much."

"I know, but Abby doesn't look so hot. I think she may be sick, Easton, and you all have families you need to go back to." I drop my gaze. "They're probably worried since they haven't heard from you."

"Hey"—he lifts my chin—"I'm worried about *you* right now."

"What happened to 'be unpredictable'?" I smile, thinking about our time together right before we were taken away from my room at the Shady Rest.

"That was before we were driven into the side of a mountain." He smiles and puts both arms around me through the tight space. He kisses me softly then Lewis clears his throat.

"One, it's time to go. We have to get to the training center," he says.

I step away and leave Easton standing at the bars. "I'll come back as much as I can. I love you."

"I'll be here," he says with a small grin.

I try to smile back and hope I'm faking it well enough. The thought of leaving them all here turns my blood to ice. How will I ever free them?

CHAPTER TWENTY-FOUR

ON OUR WAY TO THE MAIN PART of the facility I'm thinking about Easton's advice. I can't stop thinking about what he said when it dawns on me I'm walking with a 'Mr. Lewis' now. "Lewis?" He doesn't stop walking.

"Yes, One?" He glances in my direction.

"I worked for a Mr. Lewis before coming here. He owned a diner at a truck stop."

"I know." His response is curt and quick. He keeps his eyes forward.

"Why?" I ask, watching him from the corner of my eye.

"Why what?"

"Why did you know? Why would they tell you that?"

He twitches his shoulders like his uniform is full of ants. "I was there... briefly."

I stop walking, forcing him to stop as well. "You were there?" When he doesn't make eye contact but grabs me by the arm and begins pulling me along beside him again, I guess the reason and yank my arm from his hand, digging in my heels to try to keep him from walking on.

"You knew him, didn't you? Were you related to him, Lewis?"

His sigh says it all. "Yes, One, he was my grandfather—to my shame!"

" 'To your shame?' Mr. Lewis was one of the nicest, kindest, most caring men I've ever met?" My cheeks burn with anger. "Did you help kill him? Did you?" I press my hand to my leg to keep Lewis from seeing how angry I really am.

"My grandfather was a traitor to our organization, to our commander! He had a gift that he refused to use. Do you know what I would give to have inherited his gift?" His eyes flash. "It's not bad enough he retired," he says the word with disgust, "then he refused to finish one final job! Even when I practically begged him." Throwing his hands up, he looks over my shoulder into a distant memory then shakes his head. "What a waste!"

"You killed your own grandfather? How could you do that?" Tears well in my eyes and threaten to overflow.

He pulls his gun. "Go," he orders, ignoring my question and motioning me forward. "I have to get you to the training center."

We don't speak again as we wind our way back. Eventually, we end up in a huge room outfitted with an assortment of training gear. Mats hang from the walls and cover the floor. Mirrors line one wall, workout equipment and punching bags opposite from it. In the far end, clearly separated from the normal gym stuff, stand man-shaped dummies. The dummies show considerable damage as though they have been abused a lot, and at the top of the room is a set of windows separating some sort of viewing room from the facility, like club seating in a stadium.

"Sit," Lewis commands. I glare at him, but like a faithful dog, I drop to the floor, legs and arms crossed. "Commander Matthews will be here soon." Lewis holsters the gun but remains beside the door.

I wait impatiently for what seems like an eternity before the door opens again to reveal Hoyt. His dead eyes find me, and he smiles.

"Well, Vivian, I hope you haven't been bored," he says, beguilingly.

"Yeah, I'm touched by your concern. You must have been worried sick."

"Sarcasm doesn't become you, my dear. Perhaps you would do well to remember where you are." His smile vanishes. "Shall we begin?" He gestures up with his hand.

"What exactly are we beginning?" I stand.

"Your training. I need to see what you can do so that I will know how to best use your abilities." He moves to the far side where the dummies stand blindly awaiting their fate, just like me.

"You mean so you can know best how to use *me*." I know I'm playing with fire here, but I can't help myself. He brings out the worst in me.

"Touché." He rolls a dummy about five feet from me. "Now, fire a shot at the dummy, Vivian." He again motions with his hand.

I raise my brows. "Which dummy would that be? I see so many." I wave my hand around the room to include Lewis and Hoyt. He is obviously not amused judging by the tight line of his mouth, and I roll my eyes. "How am I supposed to do that? I thought I couldn't use my powers in the facility because of the equalizer doohickey." I deliberately don't tell him that I've already been using them this morning. What he doesn't know might hurt him, at least I hope so.

"In this room your powers will work." As proof, he extends both hands, and a gust of warm air tosses the dummy into the air then slams it against the wall.

"What exactly are your powers anyway?" I say, trying not to look intimidated.

"I am an Element as are you, my dear. An Element is a person who possesses an ability connected to nature, concentrated nature. I am an Air Element. My power comes from and imitates the wind. Ferguson's comes from the earth. Your power, well, your power is unusual. In fact, you are a Double-Element. You can control energy, natural and manmade, which I've never seen before, *and* you are a Water Element as well, which I've only seen one other time."

"Wait, I'm confused. I know about the energy thing but water? You're wrong. I've never controlled water." I shake my head. It's bad enough to be a freak, but a double freak is beyond enduring.

"My dear"—he chuckles as though we're old friends sharing a joke—"you most definitely are a Water and Energy Element. The energy comes from your mother. The water..." He looks away as though he can see the past at the far end of the room. "That is all your father. And don't argue with me." He faces me again and points his finger.

My father? I've wanted to know about him for so long! And this monster has given me a tiny glimpse into who my father is or was. Suddenly, it doesn't really matter that I'm a double freak. I have a gift from my father, and that makes me feel closer to him in some strange way. "But I've never controlled water before. How would you know if you've never seen me use it?"

He laughs, like a genuine, loud guffaw. "Really, Vivian? Last year, when you had that huge power-surge, where were you?"

I think back, remembering that night. We'd been fishing at the lake and having a great time when Trista and her goons showed up, including Abby who hadn't spoken to me in days. She had seen me produce an energy orb in my sleep, and it had totally weirded her out. She had buddied with Trista because of Dillon, who was playing her in order to be part of Trista's group. Trista had told Easton what a freak I was, and I had run off into the woods where I had a little lightning powwow.

"In the woods," I reply smugly. "Guess that doesn't prove anything, huh?"

"Yes, but where in the woods?" He steps in closer.

Then I see it clearly in my mind, and I realize—"By a lake," I finish quietly.

"Yes, your body instinctively took you there. Have you not noticed the rain, my dear? When you are"—he pauses and motions his hand in the air, like he's trying to catch the right word—"emotional, it rains? Think back. After you met the boy, did it rain considerably?"

Crap! He's right! At the library when I thought he would kiss me, at the lake when he did kiss me, when I left him to go for Aunt Charlotte, and almost every day since he's been back in my life. Then when we came here, the rain when I restarted the van and the comments of both Ferguson and Wallis when we approached the cave wall where the moisture was so great.

"No"—my voice shakes as my pulse quickens—"that's crazy! Who could possibly make it rain? I mean, we're talking about *the entire sky*!"

"Yes, my dear, your ability is beyond any I've ever seen—even your father's. It must have to do with the joining of both of your powers. Your mother knew. She was the only one who truly understood it then."

"You mean the mother you forced into suicide?" I growl out between gritted teeth.

"She knew. She knew the river would help protect you, would allow her to tap into some of your power, too. That's why she took you there when we were so close to taking you both. Do you think she could ever have made that energy tornado without your ability, too?"

My breathing is shallow and fast. Rage is overtaking the shock. "How dare you bring her up? You don't have the right to talk about her! Ever!"

"Really, Vivian! How will I educate you if you react this way?" He acts before I have the chance, throwing me in the same way he threw the dummy. I slam into the mirror, shattering it. He pins me there, my palm flat against the broken fragments which cut into my back and arms.

He clucks his tongue and shakes his head. "Now see what you forced me to do? I have so much to tell you, but I think we are done for today." He releases me, and I slide down landing on my butt. Every part of me aches. I don't even have the force to fire back at him.

He approaches, takes my arm, and lifts the shredded sleeve of my uniform. My wrist is a mangled mess; serious cuts and blood cover it. I wince when he yanks out a piece of glass embedded deeply near my wrist. Blood drips onto the mat beneath me. I'm pretty certain I'm going to bleed to death when the cut begins to close, knitting itself together.

"Yes, as I thought. You are also a Healer, Vivian. Another gift from your father," he says shaking his head. "You certainly are a powerful girl. You will be my shining star." He drops my wrist and walks away.

When he gets close to the door, Lewis stands at attention. "Lewis, remove the glass and allow her to heal completely before returning her to her room. Stay in the training center until she is finished. If you remove her too soon, her ability will be blocked by the equalizers that Carter installed last night." He glances back at me. "I need her healthy. Allow her to eat her evening meal with the twins." The door slides open, and he walks away.

Lewis walks briskly to a refrigerator built into the wall beside the mirrors. He grabs a bottle of water then kneels beside me and turns me around so that my back is facing him. "Lie down, One," he says, pulling gloves and some kind of tool from his uniform. He folds the handles of the tool around until pointed ends like pliers appear.

I reluctantly lie on my stomach, knowing he's the only one who can help me right now. When he rips my uniform open to expose my back, I call out from the pain.

"Sorry," he mumbles. "You're already healing around the glass fragments, so this is gonna hurt—a lot." He pours water over my back.

As he pulls out the first shard, I bite down on my lip. He continues methodically removing the pieces for what seems an eternity.

"Okay, think that's it," he says. Sweat covers my body, and my shaking this time if from pain, not anger. "Now your legs."

As he again rips my uniform, I groan. "It'll be alright, One. There aren't as many in your legs."

I cry in earnest this time.

CHAPTER TWENTY-FIVE

LEWIS RETRIEVES A UNIFORM from a closet near the door of the training center. "Here." He hands it to me and turns his back.

After he finished with my legs then my arms, I feel shaky but better. All that remains of the wounds are red welts which are disappearing, too, but my uniform is mangled beyond decency. I slip on the new one.

"Ya know, it's probably not smart for you to turn your back on me in here. Gentlemanly, yes, smart, not so much." I zip the front and sit to put my boots back on.

He turns around. "You won't hurt me."

"Oh really? You're so sure of that." I raise one finger, ticking off reasons to juice him up. "One, you are my captor. Two, you just caused me a great deal of pain. Three, and most important, you killed my friend, Mr. Lewis."

He raises his hand to count off as well. "One, I have been ordered to be your captor. Two, you would never have healed without my help. Three, things aren't always the way they seem. Maybe you don't know as much as you think you do, One."

I put both hands on my hips. "Yeah, enlighten me then."

He turns and starts for the door. "You wouldn't believe me anyway. You've got your mind all made up about me, about my grandfather, about the Liaisons." He stops and waits for me in front of the door.

"So change my mind." We leave the training center and begin our trek back to my room.

Lewis nods to several men we meet in the hallways but doesn't speak again until he opens my door with the keypad. After I'm inside, he turns to me.

"Well? I can't wait to hear this." I keep my voice bland when really I'm about to pee my pants to find out some more info.

"Well, for starters, you don't know anything about what we do here. You have to be invited to join this force. Don't roll your eyes! I was invited because of my grandfather's connection to the Liaisons." He pauses and studies his feet. "Commander Matthews thought I might have inherited his abilities, but when I didn't manifest any power, he kept me anyway."

"What exactly do the 'Liaisons' do?" I move to the arm chair, prop my feet on the ottoman, and take off my boots.

"We're a secret organization. We're the group the government calls when a situation requires special care—unofficial and top secret. We are the Extrasensory Vital Information Liaisons," he says, puffing out his chest.

"E. V. I. L.? Seriously? You are actually telling me that you work for a group called EVIL? That's about the corniest thing I've ever heard! Is that how they sign your paycheck?" I snort a laugh.

His face tightens defensively. "Don't laugh, One. You work for them now, too. We're a lot stronger than you think. The Liaisons have been around for a long time. My grandfather didn't even know exactly how long, but he was a young teenager when he joined, and it was well-established already then. Anyway"—he draws out the word and glares at me to be serious when I laugh again—"our job is to secure situations when all other options have been exhausted, but since we're a secret group, we have to stay under the radar as much as possible. We do what no one else can do."

"So, when Hoyt and I destroyed what was left of a public park, that wasn't exactly following regulations?" I cock an eyebrow at him, but he continues without acknowledging me.

"We find recruits from all over the United States, people like you and my grandfather, people with abilities beyond normal. Most people join freely. They jump at the chance to feel useful and lead exciting, fulfilled lives. Typically, those people don't really have friends and regular jobs anyway because of their abilities." He crosses his arms smugly as though he's just imparted some great wisdom instead of regurgitating crap he's been told by a psycho commander.

"You sound like a damned recruiting video! 'Those people?' You mean me? I did have a normal life with friends and a regular job until you guys came along, and I'll bet this isn't the first time your amazing commander has kidnapped someone in order to get what he wants! Come to think of it, your grandfather was an integral part of my regular life. Right before you killed him!" I stand and clench my fists, trying to control my temper.

Lewis approaches quickly and comes within inches of my face. "I didn't kill anyone. I loved my grandfather. I begged him to finish the job he'd started so that he wouldn't be killed. Yes, I was there at the end, but I didn't do it, and I sure didn't watch!"

"What job, Lewis? Help me understand all this!" I gesture around in frustration.

"Grandfather was a Magnet; that was his gift. He could attract people to him, draw them like a magnet to metal. He lured you in and kept you there until we came," he explains, sighing.

The force of that comment hits me like lead. Mr. Lewis, a man I trusted and cared for, was playing me. Did he ever really care about me like he seemed to? I slump back into the armchair and put my head in my hands.

"I'm such an idiot. I walked right into your hands," I mumble through my fingers. "Tell me something, did you all get a big kick out of how gullible and stupid I was—am?" Dropping my hands, I stare at the chocolate-brown swirls in the rug beneath my feet. If only I could melt right into that rug.

Lewis sits on the arm of the chair. "Listen, One, it wasn't like that for him. He didn't want to help them. He'd been retired for years, running that diner. He loved it," he says hanging his head. "They… we… threatened someone close to him to get him to cooperate, and he did for a while, but he refused to complete his assignment."

"And you're okay with that? Do you hear yourself? You work for a group that *threatened* someone! You work for a group that *kidnaps* and *kills* people!" I jump up again and face him.

"We protect the world! Isn't it worth hurting one person to keep the rest safe? Grandfather had gone soft! He'd forgotten how truly bad people are."

"Like me?" I walk away from him toward the door. "Leave, Lewis."

He throws up both hands in surrender. "I give up! Most people with gifts *want* to help!" He stomps to the door. "You're impossible. And no, not like you. In fact, that's why he stopped cooperating. He made the biggest mistake for someone in our line of work. He started liking his mark, and he knew you were running from Commander Matthews, but not why."

As he opens the door, I respond, "He killed my mother, Lewis. This awesome group that you belong to killed my mom."

He turns his head and looks down at me. For the first time I realize how truly young he is. His dark eyes look sincere, like he really believes everything he's saying.

"Your mother was wrong to run. You belong here, Vivian."

CHAPTER TWENTY-SIX

AROUND 6:00 PM, Wallis knocks on my door and announces he's taking me to dinner.

"I'm not hungry." I don't bother getting out of bed where I've been lying since Lewis and I had our argument.

"I don't care." Wallis moves toward the bed. "You're supposed to meet the twins at dinner whether you eat or not. Those are my orders, and you're going."

"Wallis" — I sit up and pull a pillow to my chest like it's my anchor to the world — "I know I'm an Element and a Healer, and Mr. Lewis was a Magnet, but what else is there? I mean, are there other kinds of powers?" I've developed a strange kind of trust in Wallis, and if anyone will explain it, I think he will.

He stands pensively for a minute as though he's debating whether telling me is a good idea or not.

"Please tell me, Wallis. I don't want to meet anyone until I know everything there is to know. I'm tired of feeling like an idiot." I throw down the pillow and move to the chair where my boots are.

"Well, I guess it can't hurt to tell you. It's not against my orders, and you're going to find out eventually, right?"

"You asking me?" I pull on my boots and begin to re-lace and tie them.

He quirks his lips. "You're so annoying. I feel like I'm stuck guarding my little sister," he says rolling his eyes. "There are five

known types of Gifted: Elements, like you, Ferguson, and the commander; Magnets, like Mr. Lewis; Healers, again like you; Twisters,
and Magicians." When I open my mouth to ask him to explain, he
holds up his hand to silence me. "I'm getting there. Twisters can
manipulate time. The twins you're meeting are Twisters. Well, one
is. The other has yet to manifest any powers. Magicians can create
illusions. They can make people see what they want them to see. We
have a Magician here, but she's very volatile. I try to avoid her as
much as possible. In fact, I'm not sure anyone but the commander
has much contact with her."

"So the twins are prisoners here, too?" I ask, approaching him
while finger-combing my curls.

"No, the twins came voluntarily. They understand the impor-
tance of the work we do. They're still in training, like you, but
they've been here longer. And *unlike you*, they are cooperative and
unguarded." He sneers as he opens the door for me.

"Maybe they aren't as smart as I am, or maybe they've never
watched a family member die."

"They have watched a family member die, Vivian. Their father was
killed by terrorists in an attack on the government building where
he worked—an attack we could have stopped. When Commander
Matthews approached them and their mother, they jumped at the
opportunity to join." He leads me back to the mess hall area.

"Is that supposed to make me feel bad?"

"No, but it should make you think. Your mother chose to—do
that. We didn't kill her."

"Die, Wallis, she chose to die rather than allow you to take us.
Let's just not talk at all anymore, okay?" I step through the doors
into the mess hall. I like Wallis, and I don't want to think about him
on the dark side.

"So, where are these twins?" I turn toward him, avoiding the eyes
of the people around me.

"Get a tray then I'll take you to them," he says filling his own plate.

"Isn't it unprofessional for the guards to eat with the prisoners?"
I grab a bottle of water and follow him out again.

"Since either Lewis or I have to be near you at all times, we have
no choice. Maybe if you're a good girl and do what you're told, we
can get away from each other."

"You could help me escape, and then all this would be over a whole lot faster." I smile as innocently as possible, but he just grunts out a laugh.

"I won't hold my breath."

"Me either," I reply, and he gives me a real smile. How did a guy like him get involved with these killers? I want to ask, but before I can, I realize we're heading back down the hall where my room is. "Wait. I thought I was meeting the twins."

"You are. Their room is two down from yours." He stops in front of a room without a keypad and knocks.

A chipper male voice calls out, "Come in." Wallis opens the door.

I had expected to see two identical faces, but to my surprise, the two boys don't even look enough alike to be in the same family. One boy is fair, tow-headed with alabaster skin as perfect as fine china. With his short, ultra-blond hair, he looks so honest, so pure— all-American boy meets seraphim. I'm disappointed not to find snowy white wings peeking out behind him.

The other face is anything but angelic. Angel meet devil. Though his face is as finely sculpted as his counterpart, this boy's look is sinful with shoulder-length curls of chestnut. Even in this dim light, it's easy to see hints of gold and red nestled in those locks that most girls would kill for. His dark skin reminds me of Easton's, which brings on an avalanche of guilt for noticing.

Fire and ice. The only similarity that these two share are striking indigo eyes, the color of new, dark-washed jeans.

The blond, who is dressed in the same black uniform as most of us, jumps to his feet, bumping the table where they sit and rattling their dinner trays and drinks. A welcoming smile on his otherworldly face, he rushes over, takes my tray, and thrusts it into Wallis's hands.

"You must be Vivian." He pulls me into the kind of hug you give a friend you haven't seen in a while.

Patting him once awkwardly, I glance over his shoulder to see his brother roll his eyes and shake his head.

"I'm Griffin." He pulls away but drags me by the hand to the table. "This is Wyck. We've been dying to meet you!"

Wyck the Wicked lifts his chin in a brief greeting and leans back assessing me. He knows how attractive he is in his worn jeans and t-shirt, and I'll bet I'm not the first girl he's made feel uncomfortable. I tug at my uniform and shift from foot to foot, trying not to meet his probing gaze. Butterflies hatch in my belly, and I run my hands nervously through my hair.

Griffin, oblivious to my immense discomfort, chats merrily while he pulls out a chair for me. "When Commander Matthews told me you'd be eating with us, I was so happy I'd finally get to meet you." Wallis sets my tray in front of me and joins us at the table, giving me a wink before focusing on his meatloaf and potatoes. "He says you're super-powerful, a Double-Element *and* a Healer." He shakes his head in awe and grins even bigger than before. "Wow! He said they even had to change the equalizer to help you."

"To 'help' me?" I ask, eyebrows raised.

"Yeah, he said that you're just having a few control issues because you're so powerful and that we all have to help you harness your abilities for the greater good." He nods.

Is this kid for real? I hate to burst his 'we are the future' pleasure bubble so soon after meeting him. He might, after all, come in handy if—when—I manage to get us all out of here. Wallis gives me a warning glance across the table.

"How long have you guys been here?" I ask, sipping my water and feigning interest in my meal.

Not surprisingly, Griffin responds, "About six months. Our dad was killed by terrorists while he was working for the government." He drops his gaze for the first time. "When Commander Matthews approached our mom about joining, she let us decide." He grips his fork tightly, his eyes looking into some horror from his past. "He said we'd go after those men as soon as we get the intel on exactly who they are, and we would get to use our powers to help destroy them. Keep other families safe."

"*Your* power." Wyck speaks for the first time, his deep voice causing me to jump a little. When I look at him, he's still staring at me, and I feel a whole lot like I did in high school whenever I had to speak in front of a group. My stomach butterflies morph into bats, blood-sucking, claw-your-face bats.

"Don't be like that, Wyck. Commander Matthews says it's just a matter of time till you manifest. He says one twin usually gets the power first, but the other will eventually." Griffin tilts his head and gives Wyck a sympathy nod.

"Yeah, eventually," he mumbles without taking his eyes from mine. "So, how long you had yours?" he asks, and for a second those blue eyes seem to probe my soul and leave me jumbled and incoherent.

"My what?" I eventually squeak out, sounding more like an insecure seventh grader than the tough girl I want to appear.

"Your power." He annunciates each syllable slowly. I feel really stupid, which isn't a pleasant feeling BTW and which is beginning to piss me off. I'd love to brainjack him, hear what he's thinking right now, but I'm too afraid to try. If these guys can somehow feel my presence inside their heads, the jig is up. Griffin will crap himself trying to get to the great Commander Matthews and spill the beans.

Smoldering face aside, Wyck is starting to give off a sullen bully vibe. My turn to stare at him, lips tight. If he wants to be a jerk, I can definitely accommodate him.

"All my life," I answer then turn to Griffin, deliberately slighting him to make him feel as bad as he's making me feel. "You?"

From the corner of my eye, I see Wallis hide a smile behind his napkin, probably glad I'm giving someone else a hard time instead of him.

"Only a year or so. It started around my seventeenth birthday." He smiles. "You've always known? Cool, but I guess you would since you're so powerful." His cheeks go red with embarrassment.

"What can you do anyway, Griffin? Wallis told me you're a Twister. You go around destroyin' small towns in the Mid-West?" I sample my meatloaf.

Missing my joke entirely, he enthusiastically shakes his head. "No, we can control time."

"You can." Wyck huffs, scraping back in his chair and getting up from the table. He paces to the gas fireplace. (Note to self: Their room is way better than mine. Whine to Wallis later.)

"*We* can manipulate time. I can reverse time for about ten seconds. I know it doesn't sound like much, but before coming here it was only a couple of seconds. I like to call it my 'undo' button."

At my confused expression, he continues. "You ever make some stupid, little mistake that you wish you could take back? Stick your foot in your mouth and say something really wrong? Wouldn't you like to take it back? Well, you can with an undo button, as long as it happened ten seconds ago." He grins and shrugs before turning serious again. "If I'd been there, been able to do something, I could have saved my dad. That's why the Liaisons are so important. Don't you agree?" He looks so damn eager—just as brainwashed and naïve as Lewis.

"I... well—" I'm floundering for the correct answer. If this kid's for real with his guts and glory spiel, I will probably never convince him otherwise anyway.

"Don't you want to see it?" Wyck, my unlikely savior, asks from his post near the fire. When I look at him over my shoulder, he has a cocky leer on his treacherous face, and the double meaning of his comment doesn't escape me.

"Looks and humor, the total package. Get many takers on that offer?" I sneer back. He saunters toward me again, wearing that same expression, giving me chills just a little bit.

But Griffin draws my attention back to him. "Oh yeah, all the time! When people find out what we can do, they always want to see it work," he says with innocent sincerity.

Wyck leans in close. "Yes, Vivian, people want to see *the power* all the time. We are talking about the same thing here, right?" He gives a toe-curling a smile, and I realize that he isn't as powerless as he thinks. He seems pretty dangerous to me, and I need to stay as far from his charms as possible. He's the kind of guy that promises heaven and delivers hell, like his looks have been manufactured for his personality. As he moves away, his tone becomes less sensual and more sullen. "What *you* can do, Griffin."

"I'll show you how it works when we train tomorrow, Vivian. Commander Matthews said we'll be training together in the morning. When we get to the training center, the block will be off, and I can show you what I do. Hey! Maybe you'll show me some of your tricks?"

"Yeah, sure, Griffin." In some strange way, this sweet guy weirds me out. Maybe I'm just paranoid, but Aunt Charlotte always used to say that if something is too good to be true, better check the price tag because you can't afford what it's going to cost you sooner or later.

Least his brother's a jerk from the get go. I know where I stand with someone like him. But for now, I'll make nice and hope my sixth sense is wrong.

Wallis stands and collects both our trays. "Let's go." He walks to the door.

"Aw, can't she stay a little longer, Wallis? We can play a game or listen to music or something," Griffin asks.

"Yeah, Vivian, stay. I'd love to play a game with you." Wyck's reclining on one of the two beds. He doesn't smile, just looks intense, and I inwardly thank Wallis. Even though I'm supposed to have this tremendous power, I feel like a prize turkey at Thanksgiving when he looks at me.

"No, she's had a long day, and you all need to get up early tomorrow for intense training. We have a mission soon, and Commander Matthews wants all of you to go along." Wallis sets the trays outside the door and speaks into his wrist radio.

"A mission? What does that mean?" But Wallis is already in the hall, the door closed behind him.

"We go along, help if we can." Griffin shrugs. "I've only been on a couple. The last time was less than a week ago."

"Less than a week ago?" My mind returns to the diner, to the motel, to Mr. Lewis.

"Yeah, I only got to get out of the van once, but it was a legitimate mission," he says opening the door for me.

Dread fills my chest, but I have to ask. "What did you do?"

He suddenly seems embarrassed again. Face reddening, he drops his eyes and quirks his mouth. "It was nothing really. I just stood in some guy's driveway and did my thing, reversed time ten seconds, got back in the van, and came back here."

He was there. He doesn't have to confirm it. I know. He was at Mr. Lewis's house.

Mistaking my silence for awe at his usefulness, Griffin hastens to add, "Oh, it wasn't a big deal or anything, but Commander Matthews said that I helped him save one star and catch another, whatever that means." He finishes with another lift of his shoulders.

I lock eyes with Wyck over Griffin's shoulder. He scrutinizes my face, his dark brows drawn together, his head tilted as though he can see how important this information is. I mask my emotions and try to smile at Griffin.

"I'll see you tomorrow." I'm trying to sound as cheerful as possible while my dinner surges into my throat.

"Okay, maybe I'll see you at breakfast first." He nods his head.

As I close the door, I hear Wyck, "Can't wait, Vivian."

CHAPTER TWENTY-SEVEN

I'VE LAID AWAKE MOST OF THE NIGHT thinking about Griffin's role in Mr. Lewis's death and my eventual capture. Could Hoyt have used Griffin to *save* Mr. Lewis? Did he shoot Mr. Lewis so that he had a vivid memory to give me then use Griffin to reverse time and bring Mr. Lewis back? That had to be what he was doing.

I'm already dressed by the time Lewis knocks then enters my room. He nods, but I turn my back to ignore him while I pull my hair into a sloppy bun. I haven't forgotten our last conversation about his grandfather and my mother.

He clears his throat as I'm lacing and tying my boots then shuffles awkwardly from foot to foot until I finally glance his way. "Look," he says, "I know you're angry, but eventually, you'll see I'm right. This group is important, Vivian. You have a gift I would do anything to have! Why can't you understand that it's your duty to use it and help us?" He puts his hands on his hips and shakes his head. He truly believes in this crap he keeps spouting. I wonder if he knows about Griffin's role in his grandfather's death. There's one way to find out for sure.

Stepping close to him, I put both hands on his face to make the strongest connection possible. His eyes widen. "What are you doing, One?" Within the space of a single breath, he drops his arms loosely to his sides and stares vacantly ahead as I enter his mind and rapidly sort through his memories to find that day.

When I close my eyes, I see what he saw. Mr. Lewis, beaten and bloody, kneels on the floor of his basement. He's shaking his head. "I know you don't understand right now, Tyler, but someday you will. I was just like you once," he says. "I believed in the Liaisons, wanted to do everything I could to help. But over the years, I figured out some things, did some things that were just wrong. I retired to try to forget. And I've been happy until I discovered that you were with them. I should've known Matthews would recruit you, hopin' you had inherited the gift." He reaches out his wrinkled hand and touches Lewis's cheek. "Boy, you have to get away from them. Run, hide, change your name, leave everything behind before it's too late. Don't you see he's only usin' you to get to me?"

Lewis jerks away. "No! I'm useful, Grandpa! He needs me! And maybe I'll manifest and become a Magnet like you soon, but until then, I'll do everything he asks of me. I want to be like you, help people all over the world. Why can't you see *that*?" He rubs at his eyes, wiping away tears. "Do what he asks, Grandpa. Then you can come back with us. We can work together!"

But Mr. Lewis shakes his head. "I can't, Tyler. I won't. If this is my last stand, then so be it, but I won't help him trap that girl. I've already done more than I wanted to do. She's a good person, Tyler, feisty and strong." He smiles sadly. "Reminds me so much of her mother." His expression turns grim again. "I wish I'd never agreed to draw her in the first place. But I'll do what I can to fix this now."

"He'll kill you, Grandpa." Lewis lurches to his feet. "Please, for me. Just do this thing! I believe in our cause, and we need her. But I need you more. Please"—he kneels again—"just bring her to him and be done with this."

I feel Lewis's conflict, his struggle to save his grandfather but stay loyal to a man he believes is saving the world and his fear that his grandfather may be right about Hoyt using him.

"I'm sorry, Tyler. I can't." Mr. Lewis bows his head. "Leave now, son. Don't stay for what happens next. It'll make me stronger knowin' you aren't seein' this happen."

Lewis pulls the old man to him and holds him briefly then walks away without a second glance.

After he walks out of the house, he sits down in the passenger seat of a van parked in the driveway, and the driver, a man I think

I've seen in the mess hall, pulls away from the house and past a second van parked on the street.

I drop my hands from Lewis's face, thinking of how much this kid—and he is really only a kid—has been through. He lost his grandfather, and he really had begged him to finish his work. Despite what he says or the tough guy image, he was hurt by his grandfather's death as much as he was by what he considered a betrayal to his precious cause. I've been so angry that I haven't stopped to think about his pain, pain that I of all people understand completely. If Mr. Lewis was right, Hoyt was just using Lewis to convince his grandfather to stay with the organization. That brief time in his head was enough to let me feel all of his conflicting emotions and long enough to make me feel guilty for being such a bitch to him.

He blinks, trying to make sense of his few lost minutes. "Uh... What was I saying?" he asks, brows drawn close together.

"Nothing, we were just leaving." I walk around him toward the door.

He remains in the same spot for a second then quickly steps in front of me to open the door. Before we walk out into the hall, I turn to him. "I'm sorry for what happened to your grandfather, Tyler, and I'm sorry for thinking that you didn't care about him. I know that you didn't kill him." Even though I'm not usually all touchy-feely, I can't help tiptoeing and wrapping my arms around his thin shoulders.

When I step away, I give him a quick, sympathy smile. With a shocked expression, he replies, "Uh ... thanks, I guess." He clears his throat. "Let's go, One."

About halfway to the mess hall, he stops walking and looks quizzically down at me. "How did you know my first name?"

Crap! Thinking fast and relying on Lewis's simplicity, I reply, "Wallis must have said it."

"Oh, yeah, okay. But you should probably not call me that again." His expression's uncertain but accepting.

"Of course, sorry, Lewis." I salute. "Wouldn't want to confuse you for a real-life human being." I roll my eyes, trying to hold onto that empathy I felt earlier and remember Lewis is just a hurt kid.

After a quick trip through the buffet line, we eat in silence then hurry to the training center. The first person I see as we step into the large room is Wyck. He is shirtless, wearing only athletic shorts and tennis shoes, and he's sending punch after punch into a large bag hanging from a chain in one corner. I try not to notice the sheen of sweat covering his chiseled torso or the way his muscles bunch as he twists around to where we stand by the door. I ignore the dark blue of his eyes and indecent fullness of his lips. Who am I kidding? He's an ass, but he is definitely sexy. Guilt slams me like a city bus, and I force my gaze away.

"Well, if it's not Princess Vivian. I wasn't sure you'd really show up to demonstrate your greatness to the poor peasants," he sneers, unwrapping athletic tape from around his knuckles and tossing it down.

"Didn't realize I had a choice." I move toward the dummies across the room. I at least need to pretend not to ogle him. Lewis remains standing by the door, legs apart, arms behind his back, like the soldier he believes himself to be.

Wyck follows me, slinging sweat from his drenched hair. "Sure, your highness, you always have a choice." He approaches me from behind while I try to pull the heavy dummy away from the others and closer to the center of the room. My clumsy efforts don't get me too far before the thing tips on its rollers and leans precariously toward me. A girly squeal embarrassingly slips out as I throw up both hands to steady it.

Wyck reaches out sighing and lifts it easily up again. "You're the chosen one, right?" He pulls it the rest of the way to the center of the room and locks the wheels.

"Where's Griffin?" I ask, feeling my temper rising along with my blush.

"He'll be here. He's gone to retrieve the lovely Lilah." Wyck steps back from the dummy then delivers a roundhouse kick to the side of its synthetic head.

"Who's Lilah?" I hope the sudden heat I'm feeling has to do with the room's temperature and not the nearness of this boy.

He laughs wryly and punches the dummy's stomach. "You'll see."

"Why are you here?" I sit down on the mat and stretch my legs in front of me, leaning on my arms behind me.

He stops his attack on the defenseless dummy and glares at me. Gritting his teeth a second, he glances away and shakes his head before looking back at me. "I have no gift, so I'm useless. Is that it, princess?"

"No"—I force myself to meet his heated scowl—"okay, yeah, that's what I mean." Suddenly, I'm pissed at this guy with all his juicy hotness. He's given me nothing but attitude since I met him last night. Time to give back. "But I'm not just talking about right now—in here. I mean, why are you here with this group when you are obviously not as gung-ho-go-team as your brother is? Or is it just me bringing out this pleasant personality of yours?"

Wyck wipes the sweat from his forehead with the back of his hand and surprises me by plopping down beside me. He exhales forcefully. "I don't owe you an explanation."

"Then don't give it," I snap.

He leans in closer and raises his finger between our faces. "*But* it's been… difficult to be here and watch Griffin's power strengthen, evolve, while I"—he flips his hand toward the dummy—"beat up mannequins. Then here you come with not just one ability but three."

"That's not my fault. You're being a jerk to the wrong person," I say with a shake of my head. "I'll let you in on a little secret, Wyck. I don't *want* to be here. I'm not a joiny joiner like you two."

He tilts his head like he did last night. "Then why are you here?"

"Tell me you aren't that naïve." I stand.

Before he has a chance to answer, Griffin enters the room with a tall, brunette girl. Unlike his brother, Griffin is dressed in the same uniform I'm wearing. The girl, however, is not. Her short, red and black striped skirt, skin tight, pink baby-doll t-shirt coupled with tall pink socks and Mary Jane shoes scream anime. As she gets closer, I notice her pig-tailed hair is died black with blue streaks, and garish makeup completes her ensemble. Standing as tall as Griffin and towering over me by a good seven inches, she looks like she stepped out of a comic book.

Griffin smiles welcomingly. "Vivian! I'm so glad we're all training together today! This is Lilah."

"Hi, Lilah." I smile at the girl, but she only nods once. Her face is expressionless and stoic.

Undaunted, Griffin continues cheerfully. "Lilah is a Magician. She can create illusions and make you see anything she wants you to. Show her, Lilah," he says, turning from me to Lilah.

Rolling her eyes, Lilah huffs out a breath. "This isn't the circus, Griffin. You can't tell me to do tricks for the audience like some trained monkey."

"But that's why we're all here, isn't it? To get to know each other and what we can do?"

"No, that is *not* why I am here," she snaps. Speaking slowly like she's responding to a child, she says, "I am here because Matthews told me to be here, not as a social gathering. And if I don't want to do tricks for your new friend, then I won't."

But as soon as she says this, Hoyt's voice comes over a speaker. "Lilah, we discussed this. Play nice, and you will be rewarded."

I turn in circles, searching for the owner of the voice, but Wyck, with another eye roll, points up to the windows at the top of the room. Standing in one window is Hoyt.

"It is the circus, complete with an audience," I mumble. "And if you roll your eyes at me one more time, you'll not like the consequences." I narrow my eyes in Wyck's direction.

Lilah sighs. "Alright, let's just do this already so I can leave. I know how to use my powers. I don't need to train." She sneers that last word and looks pointedly in my direction. "Let the newbie practice after I'm done."

"Great!" exclaims Griffin, still smiling and still way too excited.

"Where are we going?" she asks with a bored expression.

Griffin glances up as though he's thinking. "New York. No wait! The coast of Maine. No!"

"Just pick a place, Griff," says Wyck exasperatedly.

"The jungle. Yeah, take us to a tropical rainforest. I've always wanted to go there." Griffin raises his brows and nods.

"Whatever." Liliah shakes her head at his enthusiasm. Then she closes her eyes and sweeps her hand almost elegantly in front of her.

In less time than it takes to blink, we're no longer in the training room. The walls are now a thick tangle of green vines and large-leafed plants. Exotic orange and red flowers bloom in sparse patches where sunlight streams through holes in the canopy above. Strange animal calls fill the air, and the heat presses down worse than a summer night back home. Sweat beads on my forehead and back.

"Wow!" exclaims Griffin, surveying the scene with awe. "Monkeys," he says, "we need some of those cute little monkeys."

Lilah, who hasn't opened her eyes, replies, "Are you sure you're not eight instead of eighteen?" But just as she utters the last word, a tiny monkey appears, the kind kids like to watch throw poop at the zoo.

"More," says Griffin.

"Yes, boss," Lilah grumbles. More of the monkeys appear, swinging merrily above us and screeching like monkeys do.

"Isn't it cool?!" Griffin shouts when one monkey dips close to his head, causing him to dunk down and laugh.

As a line of sweat runs down my back, the realism of the illusion astonishes me. I can see it, hear it. I can even smell the moist earthiness, and suddenly, I'm reminded of another dream so realistic it was shocking—the dream Easton and I shared that night at the motel. Lilah must have been there. She must have been responsible for it.

"Can you make any illusion?" I need to test my theory.

Eyes still closed she says, "Yeah, any image I can imagine."

"So do you have to have actually traveled to that place, or can you just create an image from a photograph?" The more I know about her power, the better. This is an amazingly scary ability.

"Like I already said, a picture's enough." She shakes her head in my direction.

With her smart ass comment, she's confirmed what I feared. Two of these three teenagers helped kidnap me and my friends. Immediately, my defenses go up, and the tension causes my powers to flare. I try to hide my glowing palm in my uniform pocket and pretend like every nerve in my body isn't tingling, but Wyck steps close.

"What's wrong, princess? Lilah upsetting you?" he whispers near my ear, his breath cool against the heat of my neck.

I turning my head and narrow my eyes at him a second time. "Stop calling me that."

His smile is mischievous and more than a little mocking. "I notice you didn't answer my question. Don't worry, *Vivian*"—he draws out my name—"I'll protect you if you want."

I huff out an incredulous breath. "Poor Wyck. The heat's getting to you if you think I need anything from you. In fact, I'd be okay with you not talking to me for the rest of the day." I turn away, but he only laughs.

One of the monkeys perches playfully on Griffin's shoulder while he pets it, and the realism of the dream shocks me again. It would be so easy to believe this scene is genuine. As I reach out a hand to touch one of the minute creatures myself, it screeches and bares its teeth before it swings away into the jungle. I whip my head in Lilah's direction and see her cruel sneer even though her eyes are still closed.

"How did you know—" I start to say, but she just curls her lips.

"I'm controlling this, remember? I can see it all, even you, in my head."

Then that means she saw what Hoyt did to Easton and me the night of the dream. She saw him throw us around, heard everything he said. So she knows the reason I'm here. She knows I don't want to be a part of the Liaisons, and from the harsh slant of her lips, I'm guessing she knows I've just figured all this out.

I round on her, my body shaking and temper rising. But before I can take a step in her direction, a loud roar erupts from my right. I whip around as an enormous gorilla charges toward me, his vicious yellowed fangs heading for my head. In a flash, my vision tunnels white and gray.

"Vivian!" Wyck shouts, grabbing my arm when I jerk my palm forward. He sails backward and lands on his butt as I fire a massive jolt toward the raging beast; bright blue electricity zings through the jungle leaves and blasts the gorilla in his broad chest.

The vision vanishes to the sound of Lilah's laughter. Close to the far wall, the dummy Wyck had moved for me earlier burns a bright orange. Lewis jumps into action, grabbing a fire extinguisher from the wall and rushing over to douse the flames.

"That was the funniest shit I've ever seen!" She cackles, holding her side as she doubles over in laughter.

My anger skyrockets. I'm vaguely aware of Griffin's yell and the look of shock on Lilah's face as I fling an energy rope around her upper arms and torso.

"Vivian, stop!" Griffin runs toward me but pulls up short as I jerk my head in his direction. One look at my glowing eyes, and he's backing up again. "It was a joke! She didn't mean anything by it! Right, Lilah? Tell her!"

But when Lilah opens her mouth to respond, I squeeze the rope tighter. Her face turns red, and she gasps for breath.

Wyck, back on his feet and slowly approaching me as if I'm a man-eating lion, nods his head. "Griffin's right, Vivian. Lilah scared the hell out of us when we first met her, too."

So this bitch is a bully. I hate bullies. I squeeze again. Her face kaleidoscopes from purple to blue.

"Vivian, you will stop this now," Hoyt calmly declares from his penthouse view. "I ordered her to test your reflexes."

In response, I raise my palm and the rope into the air. Her feet dangle uselessly. "I want to see him, Hoyt! I put her down, you let me see him! And I want to be allowed inside his cell, or I swear I'll crush her!"

His sigh is audible over the speaker. "Very well, my dear, Lewis will take you to him."

"Swear it! Swear it now!" I yell, yanking her even higher.

"I swear it, Vivian. Now put her down." His voice is as unruffled as ever.

For a minute, I consider being nice and letting her down gently then I remember the bloody wound in Easton's shoulder that happened in her illusion, and I drop her like a rock. She lands on her back and gasps for air as Griffin rushes over to kneel beside her. He helps her sit up while she pants heavily, and her cheeks pinken again. Eyes wide, Wyck stands blinking in astonishment.

"Sorry, Wyck. Collateral damage." I shrug and jog for the door. I've had all I can handle for one day. I can't get away from these people fast enough.

"Vivian," he calls, but I don't bother stopping or looking back. "I'll never call you princess again."

"No, you won't," I say as the door closes behind me.

CHAPTER TWENTY-EIGHT

MY MIND IS REELING. I can't wait to tell Easton everything—Lilah's role in our dream, the possibility that Mr. Lewis might be alive thanks to Griffin's power, and my Double-Element-Healer status.

Lewis interrupts my thoughts. "I've never seen anything like that, One, and I've seen"—he gives an incredulous snort—"a lot of unbelievable things!"

"Leave it alone, Lewis." I quicken my steps.

"Don't you see? That is exactly why you belong here. What you did to the dummy was one thing, but that electric rope... Lilah is not going to be happy." He chuckles as though he might actually be glad. Has this girl pissed off everybody?

"I don't want to talk about it, Lewis."

"But why not?" He's almost giddy, like a kid that's discovered a new toy.

"Lewis!" I stop and face him. "I do not want to talk about it! I just want to see Easton, okay?"

"Alright, alright, sorry," he says, taking a step back. Guess my performance has made an impression on Lewis. We continue on in silence until we reach the sliding panel concealing the prisoners' cells.

I pause at the cell occupied by Cooper and Abby, but it's empty. Just as my fear threatens to choke me, Easton calls out, "Vivian? Vivian!"

I run to his cell where he's gripping the bars. He pulls me as close as possible through the opening. "I knew it was you. I felt you before you opened the door." He kisses me hard on the mouth.

"Easton, where are they? What's happened?" I ask when he releases me.

"The doctor sent for Abby, and Cooper refused to let her go without him. She's pretty sick. They've been gone for a while." He runs his fingers through his onyx hair.

Lewis stands close behind me. "Open the cell, Lewis," I command without looking back. "That was the deal. I get to be inside the cell with him."

He moves to the keypad, punches in a code, and the door opens. Easton jerks me inside and holds me as though we haven't seen each other in weeks instead of a day. I can't tell if the force of his grip or if his nearness is making me light-headed. For a moment, we are lost in each other. His touch ignites my senses, causes me to tremble and tingle.

Then I remember Lewis. I need time alone with Easton even if it means brainjacking him again. I move away from Easton and face Lewis through the bars. I suppose because I've connected with him more than once it's really easy to get inside his head this time.

"Lewis, take a break then check on Abby before you come back." I gaze forcefully into his eyes, which glaze over as he turns toward the door and walks away.

"Easton, I have so much to tell you! I've found out so much—" but before I can say more, he tugs me to him again. His soft lips brush mine, and I lose all conscious thought, focusing only on the connection between the two of us. One of his strong hands moves to the small of my back while the other cups the back of my head. I slide my hands up his chest and into his hair. His lips press harder against mine as he deepens the kiss.

"Vivian," he breathes against my mouth.

I tighten my grip on his hair and hold him against me. His mouth slides to my neck where he feathers kisses up to my ear and down to the erratic pulse at the base. When his hand slips from my hair to my shoulder and lower to the buttons of my uniform, the lights in the cell and hall flicker. My body is thrumming, my power amped high, and I'm involuntarily drawing the energy. Easton doesn't notice or doesn't care. His aqua eyes stare down into mine while he slips the first few buttons open, and as his fingers brush the cotton of the tank I'm wearing beneath my uniform, I inhale sharply. The lights dim to near darkness. He pushes my uniform over my shoulders and sweeps me into his arms, carrying me to his cot where he lays me down then lies down on his side next to me after yanking his shirt over his head.

I can't resist rubbing my hands up and down his defined chest and stomach. A low groan slips from his lips when I kiss his shoulder, his neck, and his sculpted pectorals. He skims his hand across my stomach and beneath my tank, his calloused fingers gliding along my ribs.

He pants in my ear, his breath warm against my ear. "This isn't the most romantic place, but—"

"I know, Easton," I whisper. He feels the pressure of this place, too. He knows we could be separated at any time, permanently if things don't go well. Despite Easton's assurance that I can be in control and make demands of Hoyt, we are really both powerless. At least I have *some* physical abilities, poor Easton has none. He is completely at the mercy of these people, and we have no idea when or if we'll get to be this close and alone again. Our lives are not our own, except right now, in this moment.

I lift my arms, and he pulls my tank over my head. His skin is warm and smooth against mine. His lips coax and tempt me, and when I think I'm about to ignite the cot, a flashlight beam spotlights us. Instinctively, I wrap us in an energy bubble that shimmers iridescent all around us.

"What the? One, what are you doing?!" Lewis's voice is at least two octaves higher than it normally is.

Easton shields me, making sure Lewis sees only his back while I hurriedly yank up the top of my uniform, cram my arms in the sleeves, and button it. The lights power back up, fully illuminating our make-out session.

Easton rubs his thumb over my cheekbones. "Anyone ever tell you how beautiful your eyes are when they're glowing?" He smiles and brushes his lips over mine.

I giggle, actually giggle like one of those girls I can't stand. "All the time," I say.

"Guess we gave Lewis a shock, huh?" he glances over his shoulder, and I get my first glimpse of Lewis who's sputtering and stammering, his cheeks bright red. He's pacing the length of the bars.

"He'll live." I run my hands over his shoulders one last time and pull the energy shield back into my body. "Oh! Easton, I didn't get to tell you anything! Close your eyes," I command and put my hands on either side of his face. Like before when I showed him Mr. Lewis's death, I upload all of the things I'd planned on telling Easton prior to kissing myself stupid.

I show him Griffin and let him hear what Griffin said about reversing time. Then I show him Lilah, her jungle creation, and exactly how I came to be here in his cell right now. I hesitate before showing him the scene with Hoyt in the training center because I know how angry he'll be when he sees how Hoyt made me into a human a pincushion, but I need him to see what my body can do. Last spring, I healed myself after the fight with Trista, but that was small potatoes compared to my injuries yesterday. I want him to know how my body can heal itself so fast. Maybe if he sees that then he won't worry about my safety as much.

Slowly, I pull my hands away and open my eyes, dreading to see his reaction. His expression is murderous. His eyes hold a dangerous glint, and his jaw is clenched tightly. He stands so quickly, the force of his rising scoots the cot a few inches. Before I can swing my legs over the side, he's gripping the cell's bars. Lewis stops pacing in front of Easton.

"Force him to let me out, Vivian," Easton growls, tension radiating from his body. His knuckles are white with the force of his hold.

Standing behind him, I try to reason with him. "Easton, it's not a big deal. He knew I would heal."

"No, he just thought you would. He wanted to test his sick theory! What if you hadn't healed? What then? You might never have recovered from that!"

"But I did. You can't go after him, anyway. You don't stand a chance against him. You'd be dead before you got within ten feet of him!" Damn, well done, Vivian! Remind your boyfriend how completely, utterly helpless he is! I'm sure that will make him calm down right away.

He turns his head to me so slowly that I think at first he isn't going to respond at all, but then he pierces me with those eyes and repeats, "Make him let me out, Vivian." His voice is deceptively calm.

"I won't. I won't risk you getting hurt—or worse!" It comes out more forcefully than I intend.

Without hesitation, he whips around, thrusts his hands through the opening in the bars, grabs an unsuspecting Lewis by the front of his uniform, and slams his head hard against the bars.

"Easton! Stop!" I scream while Lewis, recovering from his surprise, grips Easton's wrists. When Easton bangs his head a second time, Lewis, his head bleeding badly, grapples for his gun.

"No, Lewis!" I shriek and blast Lewis from Easton's hands, sending him crashing against the rock wall behind him and knocking him unconscious.

"What are you doing?" I shout as I grab Easton's arm. When he faces me, the rage in his face is shocking. He's breathing hard and shaking.

"Open the bars. I know you can. Do it!" he yells. I've never seen him this angry, not even when he found me at the diner.

"I won't do it, Easton. He'll *kill* you! Don't you see that? I don't know if I can protect you here, especially if he gets Griffin and Lilah to help him."

" 'Protect me?' You aren't sure you can 'protect me?' " He shakes his head and laughs humorlessly. Turning away, he yanks his shirt off the floor and jerks it over his head. "You have no idea what this is like for me." His quiet voice belies his intense expression. "I sit here, hour after hour, not knowing if you're okay, not knowing what he is making you do, or doing to you—and there isn't a damn thing I can do about it! Every once in a while, I hear your voice faintly in my head, but I can never exactly understand what you're saying, or I can see your face, but it's always blurry." He runs his fingers through his tousled hair. "I have to do *something*! I don't *want* you to protect me! Dying would be better than doing nothing!"

Tears burn behind my eyes. "You don't mean that. I won't let you do something stupid. I won't let you die."

He closes his eyes and breathes deeply. "Just go, Vivian." He snags my tank where it lies near the cot and tosses it to me then walks to the back wall and rests his forehead against it, completely dismissing me.

The tears flow unchecked as I put my hand against the bars and send a jolt to trick the keypad into triggering and opening. After slipping through, I slide them closed.

"I love you, Easton," I say quietly. But he doesn't answer, not even in his head.

CHAPTER TWENTY-NINE

AFTER HAULING LEWIS through the opening and convincing him that he slipped and fell from the condensation dripping along the wall and ceiling, we trudge back to my room. He presses a rag over the wound in his head.

"You better have that looked at, Lewis," I say automatically, without really caring if he does or not. Easton and I have never really had a 'don't talk to me' kind of fight before now. All I can think about is the look on his face and the anger in his eyes. I know the majority of that anger is directed toward Hoyt, but some is my responsibility. No, not some—all. If it weren't for me, Easton wouldn't be in this situation. Neither would Abby and Cooper. Abby! I forgot to ask about her! Nice. Not only am I the world's worst girlfriend, I suck as a best friend, too.

"Lewis, what did you find out about Abby?" He unlocks my room with the hand not holding onto his head as though it's going to fall off and roll away any second now.

"Abby? Oh, she's being treated for dehydration. They're moving her back tomorrow." His face has a pained expression.

"Can I see her?" I could force him to take me to her, but I feel guilty enough about Lewis's injuries. Making him do anything else tonight is out of the question.

"I'll ask Wallis, but it's doubtful, One." He motions me inside, closes the door, and relocks it.

When I get inside, I pull my crumpled tank from my uniform pocket. I can't stop myself from holding it against my face, remembering the feel of his skin against mine, his touch, his scent. I don't try to stop the tears from coming. I flop myself onto the bed for a good cry.

How could I have let everything get this screwed up? A week ago I was serving fried chicken and coconut cream pie to hungry truckers. I had a room, a car, and some sort of life, albeit a lonely one. It was *mine*, though, to go and come as I pleased. I have to get out of here and rescue Easton, Abby, and Cooper. But how am I going to do that when I can't even find my way around this labyrinth. I need a plan and an ally. I need to start tonight. Just then, Wallis knocks and announces that he's taking me to the mess hall.

"I'm not hungry. Go away." I sound like a petulant child, but I'm miserable, and I need to wallow in my self-pity for a little while.

"Not an option, Vivian. I'm coming in. Hope you're dressed," he says, unlocking the door and stepping inside.

I wipe my tears and sit up quickly but not quick enough.

"What's wrong?" he asks.

"Nothing, I just don't want to eat, okay? I want to climb in bed and forget this crappy day ever started." I collapse back on the bed, covering my face with a pillow.

"Is this because of Lilah? Lewis told me what happened with her. Hey, if it makes you feel better, she had it coming. She pushes everyone around. Guess she finally found someone to push back." I can hear the smile in his voice. When I don't respond, he yanks the pillow from my hands and tosses it to the floor.

"Come on. Are you scared to face her now? Don't tell me that one little encounter is going to send you running to your room." He crosses his arms over his massive chest and raises his brows.

Why is this guy so damn likeable? It dawns on me that maybe that's part of Hoyt's plan—pair me with Wallis, the friendly giant, and Lewis, the dumb kid.

"Please, Wallis, leave me alone tonight," I plead, sitting up and giving him a pout. I'm fully prepared to give him a mental nudge in that direction when he sighs.

"Okay, just for tonight. I'll be back later. I have to take care of some things first. Lewis wasn't supposed to need a relief until after 2200 hours." He turns to leave then stops and slowly faces me. "Hey, you wouldn't know anything about that nasty gash on his head, would you?"

From the narrowing of his eyes, I can see he knows there is more to the slip and fall story. "No, I was with Easton when it happened." I know I've messed up as soon as the words are out.

"You were alone with him? I was told you could be in his cell, not be alone with him." He crosses his arms again, but this time it's not in that playful way. It's more like he's taking a battle stance.

Think fast, Vivian. "He went to check on Abby. I begged him to go and see if she was okay," I say, surprisingly maintaining eye contact. I don't want to get Lewis in trouble, but I can't let Wallis get too suspicious of me.

He tilts his chin up, appraising me down the slope of his nose. "I'll check the footage, see if I can figure it out." He starts for the door again.

"Footage?" I squeak. "What footage?" I try for nonchalance, but he sees right through me.

"You must realize that you're being filmed everywhere you go in this facility." His look is smug as though he's caught me stealing from the cookie jar.

Shit! Not only is there footage of Easton and me in his cell, but there's also footage of Easton—okay, me, too—assaulting Lewis.

"I'll just go now before I take care of my other duties." He moves to open the door.

"Wait!" I yank him back into the room. I have no choice. Slapping my hands a little too forcefully on his cheeks, I force his mind open. Whether Wallis's memories are a piece of cake, or I'm becoming way too efficient at this, I can't tell, but it only takes a second to find this conversation and pull it out of his mind. And, since I'm already here, I might as well do some exploring. I search his mind for blueprints of this place, every hall, every room, everywhere he's been in the facility.

My handprints burn pink on his cheeks. "Thanks, Wallis. I promise I'll go to breakfast in the morning," I say, as though nothing has happened.

He looks around and rubs his face. "What were we talking about?"

"About how great you are in letting me skip dinner."

"Humph," he grunts, "I must be tired." He shakes his head and leaves without a glance back.

* * *

I wait about thirty minutes before I pop the lock and sneak a glimpse into the hall. Crossing my fingers that everyone is in the mess hall, I slip out, relocking my door in case Wallis checks it later. I don't know if the new equalizer still hasn't been installed or if I'm somehow getting around it, but I can't worry about that right now. Closing my eyes, I visualize Wallis's map. First stop has to be the surveillance room in case he gets curious about Lewis's injuries again.

Fortunately, I only meet one other person, and she is rushing, typing on a tablet, so she doesn't notice me. Three turns later, I'm standing in front of a sliding door with a keypad and a scan. I know I can get around the keypad, but the scan might present a problem. I'm racking my brain (and Wallis's memories) to figure out my options when a hand on my shoulder causes me to jump.

"What exactly are you doing?" Wyck is so close his breath stirs the loose hair beside my ear.

"Wyck! Why aren't you at dinner?" Spinning around, I nearly bump noses with him. He's still not dressed in the standard uniform but is wearing a pair of dark-wash jeans and a t-shirt. His breath is minty; his smile is lethal, like a cougar trapping a deer.

"I was just about to ask you the same thing," he sneers, leaning against the sliding door.

"I… I was… lost. Wallis had an emergency, and I told him I could find the mess hall, but"—I try to smile sweetly, innocently—"I guess I can't."

"Well, lucky for you"—he taps my nose playfully—"I can. Come on, I'll show you." He clasps my arm to lead me away, but I pull back. If I let him lead me to the mess hall, Wallis will want to know how I unlocked my door, but I don't trust this kid enough to tell him I can still use my powers. "Level with me, Vivian. Why are you here?" He crosses his arms.

"Alright." I sigh. I have to give him *some* version of the truth. "I lied. I didn't get lost. I'm snooping, okay?"

"For what?"

"I need in this room, Wyck!" When I realize how loud my voice is, I quickly scan the hall, hoping no one has heard me. "I have to see some video from earlier today. I think that video is in this room."

"Well, why didn't you say so from the beginning?" he asks, grinning roguishly. "Step aside. I may not have superpowers, but I'm a computer genius." He places his hand on the scanner, and within a couple of seconds we're inside a monitor-filled room.

"You have access to this room?" I step over to the monitors.

"I have access to almost every room in this facility, and no, it's not because I was granted access." He is once again standing way too close for comfort behind me. "We have something in common, Vivian. I like to 'snoop,' too."

"I'm impressed."

"It was easy really. While Griffin perfected his" —his face shows his jealousy—"talent, I got into one of the control computers, and the rest was easy." He sits in front of a monitor, and his fingers fly over the keys. While I watch his eyes rove over the screens as they flash in quick succession, I realize we have more in common than he knows. If he felt the need to hack into their systems, he obviously doesn't trust these people either. This may be the ally I need.

"Are you happy here?" I ask, leaning against the counter to get a good look at his face.

He stops typing and meets my gaze. "It's important to Griffin." He shrugs.

"Yeah, but what about you? Is it important to you?"

He's the first to break our stare, but he doesn't begin typing again. "I don't know. I miss home sometimes, my friends, going out with girls, parties—being a normal guy."

It's time to take a chance. "Wyck, I'm not here because I want to be. Matthews has my boyfriend and two of my friends. He kidnapped them and is forcing me to stay here."

His pursed lips and slow nod tell me he's not surprised. "I know. After what you said today in the training center, I did some research. I convinced some chick in one of the offices to go get us a soda. She couldn't resist my charm." The smile he flashes is probably the exact one he used on her. "She came back way too fast, but I did see that three prisoners were being held, and when I saw Lewis walking back from the prison quarters, I put two and two together."

"I have to get them out and escape. I'm trusting you not to tell anyone, but I have to do it soon." I crouch down so that we're eye-to-eye. "These people are not the heroes you think you are. They're killers. They killed

my mother, my Aunt Charlotte, and I think they killed Lewis's grandfather. Who knows how many people they've hurt!"

He searches my eyes. "How do I know you aren't setting me up
right now?"

" 'Setting you up?' Why would I do that, Wyck? I'm asking you
for help."

The expression on his face tells me he's decided to trust me. "I
don't think Matthews wants me here anymore," he says dropping
his gaze. "I'm not useful to him since I don't have any powers, and
I think he's afraid I'll convince Griffin to leave."

"How do you know? What happened?"

"Nothing happened… yet. It's the way he looks at me and the
way he's stopped working with me. I think he deliberately tries to
keep us apart, always calling for Griffin alone. I'm beginning to feel
like a liability."

While I've told Wyck he can trust me, I have no idea if I can trust
him. I need to see if he's telling the truth. I can't jump into this thing
without confirming his honesty. After all, I barely know this guy,
but at the same time, I don't want to spook him.

I touch his head, and he glances back up. When we lock eyes, I
dive into his mind. He is way more complex than Lewis or Wallis,
and I stay inside searching longer than I should. Wyck is arrogant,
angry, and willing to stop at nothing to protect his brother, but he's
also being completely honest with me. I move my hand and step
back. Like almost everyone I've ever brainjacked, he blinks rapidly
at first. Then he smiles.

"You just did something to me, didn't you?" He doesn't sound
mad or surprised.

"What? No, what would I have done?" I try to sell the innocent
act again, but he's not buying.

"Vivian, can you still use your powers?" he asks tilting his head
quizzically.

I sigh, no point in pretending. "Yes." I throw up my hands in
exasperation then point at him. "But if you tell anyone, I will make
you very sorry. You saw what I did today."

He puts up his hands defensively. "Hey! Don't go all ninja on
me! I didn't say I'd tell anyone. That's how you got out of your
room, huh?"

"Look, we don't have a lot of time here." I'm tired of talking. It's time to take care of this video. "I need to delete some footage from this afternoon. Will you help me or not?"

He spins around to the monitor again. "You're right. We need to hurry before dinner is over. What am I looking for?"

How do I say this? "I need right after you saw Lewis walk away from the prisoners' quarters." I feel my face heating up. "But I need you not to watch it." I stare at the screen, making sure not to look at him.

"How can I find a video without looking at it? That doesn't make any sense. Why would you want me not—" Then he smiles. "Oh, you and your little boy toy, huh? I get it." He speeds through footage until he gets close then he turns away and covers his eyes while he laughs. "Just hit the control and shift at the same time, and the video will go snowy."

I scoot in close and kneel beside his chair, but when Easton and I start to kiss, the footage goes dark then I remember how the lights had dimmed. I make it snowy anyway in case Mr. Computer Genius can somehow brighten it up.

"Are you finished, or was this an extra-long scene?" He swings back around even though I don't give him the okay.

"Yes, you can look now, but I'm not finished." I fast-forward to the part where Easton smacks Lewis's head into the bars and mess that up, too.

"Whoa! Boy toy has a temper. Better not tell him how you probed the deepest, most private parts of my psyche."

"I didn't probe your 'private parts.' Don't flatter yourself, Wyck," I say, trying to sound firm but unable to hide a tiny grin of my own. "Done."

"Now what, princess—oh sorry! Don't lasso me." He holds up his hands again.

This time I do laugh, probably the first actual laugh I've let myself have in here. "It's okay. I kind of like it."

He raises his brows. "Well, your highness, what should we do now? Spy on Lilah? She's a real freak, you know, into all kinds of weird stuff," he says with a small shudder. "Maybe look into some top secret files?"

"Files? What kind of files?"

"Personnel files. They keep records on anyone who's ever worked here. Lewis, Wallis, even me and you."

"You've seen them? Our files?" This may be my chance to find out info on my dad.

"Some of them. There are others that are so encrypted I haven't been able to break into them yet." His fingers move again as he begins opening file after file. Faces and dossiers pop up in rapid succession. Lewis and Wallis flash past.

"You can't see ours?" I lean close to the screen as if that will somehow help me find the file.

"No, none of the files on the Gifted are fully visible. I'm going to keep working on it, though. I just need to convince Patricia to help me without her realizing she is." He leans back in his chair.

"Who's Patricia?" I sit down on the floor.

"The girl who brought me a soda today," he replies with that same devilish grin.

"I'm sure it will be a great hardship." I roll my eyes and get to my feet.

Suddenly, he leaps up. "Shit!" he exclaims as he yanks me away from the screen.

"What the? Hey! What's wrong?!" I yell, trying to pull out of his grip.

"Shhh! On the monitor, look!" Before he hustles me to the back wall, I catch a glimpse of someone moving toward the surveillance room.

When we get close to the wall, he pulls open the door to a narrow, dark room filled with monitors and keyboards. As he clicks it closed, I hear the sliding door open and footsteps approaching the monitors. Since he knows I can use my powers anyway, I might as well take advantage of it. I close my eyes and speak into his head.

Wyck, can you hear me?

Because it's so dark, I can't see his shock, but I can feel him jump slightly. Then I hear a tentative voice in my own head.

You're talking in my head? How screwed up is this?

I was thinking the same thing. Where are we?

He peeks through the tiny crack he left between the door and doorjamb.

In a storage closet. This is not the first time I've had to use it.

How long do you think we'll be in here?

He doesn't reply at first. Then he settles back against the wall. It's so tight in here that he can barely stretch his legs out completely.

Until Ferguson takes a break.

Wait, did he say Ferguson? Awesome. If we're caught, I'm in a world of trouble.

You might as well make yourself comfortable. Don't worry. I doubt it will be more than a couple of hours. Ferguson's a lazy prick, and he's messing around with Lilah, so I'm sure he'll be sneaking off soon.

Ferguson and Lilah? Can anyone say 'nasty'?

I don't even want to know how you know that.

No, you probably don't. It's one of those moments I wish I could scrub from my brain.

But we don't have to wait long before Lilah herself shows up. Her voice and the clack of those Mary Janes on the tile floor are unmistakable. We hear her giggling then Ferguson grunts and from there, it's a whole lot of noises I refuse to decipher.

Wyck shifts uncomfortably, and I get the feeling he's trying to move away from me so that our shoulders and hips aren't touching, but there is absolutely no wiggle room in this cupboard. I try really, *really* hard not to enter his head, and I think he's trying to block me, but somehow it's having the reverse effect because his brain is a smorgasbord of images right now. While I'm trying not to think about what is happening in that room, Wyck can't seem to stop himself from visualizing it all in living color.

Wyck! Will you stop? I can see every thought in your twisted brain!

I'm sorry! I'm trying not to, but… I'm a guy, alright! A guy who hasn't even held hands with a girl in way too long!

You mean Patricia wasn't as eager as you thought she'd be?

Shhhh! I'm trying not to think here!

I plug my ears and squeeze my eyes closed as if that will help, and Wyck begins to sing sitcom theme songs in his head. I think it's working till he accidentally brushes my thigh with his hand. The next image isn't Ferguson and Lilah. It's the two of us, kissing.

Wyck! Stop thinking now!

But the image doesn't stop. The kissing turns to touching, the touching to undressing. His breathing turns heavy, and I can't truthfully say I'm totally *un*affected by it either. I have to stop this if he can't. So, I do the only thing I can. I zap him, a teensy-weeny zap but enough to cool him off fast. He jerks away from me what little he can in this tight place.

Damn, princess! That hurt!

Well, you wouldn't stop. You left me no choice.

But even in the dark, I can feel his smile as he relaxes beside me again.

Admit it. You were enjoying yourself too much. You liked what you saw.

No, I was... disgusted.

He snorts quietly, and a part of me is afraid he might be right.

CHAPTER THIRTY

"BRING THE SOAP AND WATER! Quickly, Ethan!" Lord St. Clair's voice shook slightly as he motioned Ethan over with a wave of his hand.

Nearly slipping again on the wet floor, Ethan rushed to Virginia's side. After setting down the water and soap, he clasped Virginia's trembling hand. He stroked her rain-dampened hair.

"'Twill be fine, Virginia. Lord St. Clair will deliver the babe, and all will be well," Ethan said, trying to believe the words.

She shook her head and gritted her teeth as the pain seized her again. "Save the babe, Ethan. Make certain he has a good home, and tell Robert about him when he returns to the colony." She hadn't told Lord St. Clair about Robert and her because she had wanted Robert to tell him, but soon it wouldn't matter. She would be dead, and Robert must know of his child.

"No! You will tell him yourself." Ethan couldn't stop the pang of jealousy at her mention of Robert. In his heart he had envisioned a life where the two of them would parent her child together.

Lord St. Clair ceased his hand washing. "What is that she said about Robert?"

Ethan glanced back at him, not wanting to utter the words he would need to say. "Robert is the babe's father, my lord. He did not know when he sailed for England."

"'Tis not possible!" he raged. "Robert would never be so reckless as to dally with a serving girl in his own home! Robert swore faith to his betrothed!"

For a moment, Virginia's agony-drenched brain cleared, and she lifted her head to look into Lord St. Clair's eyes. "His betrothed?"

"Yes, Robert has been betrothed since he was a small boy. Lady Evangeline's mother was cousin to my wife. They have known each other since they were children, running and playing together. He loves her and swore he would never forsake her! He returned to England to wed and bring her back with him."

Virginia felt as if the ground had suddenly dropped from beneath her. Robert would never be so cold, so vicious. Surely, Lord St. Clair didn't understand the love between them. He had to be mistaken. Robert had sworn his love to her. They had planned a life together.

"He... he went to England to... to settle debts for your estate," she pleaded, more to convince herself than to convince him. Even as she said the words, they suddenly sounded ridiculous.

"Debts? I haven't been to England in years. Any debt I had was settled long ago."

She squeezed her eyes closed against both the pain in her abdomen and the pain in her heart. She couldn't watch Lord St. Clair shake his head in denial. Her next scream was more than the child struggling to be born.

CHAPTER THIRTY-ONE

"**SET IT UP AGAIN!**" Hoyt's voice cuts across the carnage of the training center. He's yelling at Lewis who rushes from the far corner of the huge room to sit at a table with a tablet in front of him. He taps a few times, and the dummies and spring-loaded 'bad guys' retreat back into hiding behind the fake trees and rocks. A few of my shots have gone wild, and smoking black spots along the wall mark my failures. Poor Lewis has been practically cowering in a corner since I accidentally almost blasted off his head in the first round of this session.

But I need a break, so without waiting for permission, I plop down on the mat and lie back, out of breath. He has forced me to run this obstacle course five times since we began this training session from hell. Each time Lewis sets it up, the room goes dark, and I have to make my way from one end to the next, firing away at the cardboard terrorists or the fast-moving dummies. Every time, it's a little different, and I'm exhausted.

"Up, my dear," he announces from the safety of the viewing room.

In the past two days I've completed more courses, maneuvers, and puzzles than I would have dreamed possible in such a short time. Both Wallis and Lewis have kept their distance from me, barely speaking, delivering me to and from my room with hardly a nod. After the strange look Wallis gave me right after I stole his memory, I think he suspects something, and I wonder if he watched the footage of Lewis's 'accident.' If he did, all he saw was a snowy screen, which probably made him even more suspicious.

I haven't seen any of the others, either—not that I'm really anxious to see Wyck again after our closet time out. After Lilah and Ferguson left, we sneaked out, and I made sure not to make eye contact with him. I know it was just a 'guy' reaction, and I didn't initiate any of it, but the guilt is almost unbearable. I haven't seen Easton since our fight, and I haven't decided if I will tell him about it or not. Even though nothing happened, part of me wants to confess anyway.

"Vivian, on your feet!" Hoyt's exasperation is beginning to undo the usual unflustered sound of his voice.

"When is it Griffin's turn? You said we would be practicing together today," I call out, sitting up.

"And so you will. This is no game, so stop acting like a child. You have your first mission very soon, and I want you ready."

"You're so certain I'll fight. What if I don't?" I already know the consequences. He made it crystal clear when we began training that first day when he slammed me into the mirrors, but I refuse to be eager. I refuse to make this easy for him.

He sighs and doesn't bother to answer my question. "Lewis, begin the course," he says over the intercom.

Lewis taps the screen, but nothing happens. With a quizzical look, he taps it again. Still nothing.

"What is taking so long, Lewis?" Hoyt asks.

Lewis's face takes on a panicked expression as he hurriedly slides his fingers over the tablet. "I don't know, Commander Matthews. It isn't working. The screen shows an error message."

"Are you responsible for this, Vivian? Because this little delay will only prolong the session," Hoyt says.

"I didn't do anything! I wish I had thought of it, but I didn't." I plop back. "Guess we're done for today."

"You guess incorrectly. Lewis, radio for Carter, and tell the twins they may enter. Vivian, you will watch Griffin until the course becomes operational again."

Lewis walks to the door speaking into his wrist radio as he walks. When Griffin and Wyck enter the room, I jump up. Wyck could probably fix this glitch, but I notice he doesn't volunteer.

"Hey, Vivian, long time no see!" Griffin exclaims. He seems genuinely glad to see me as he hurries over to hug me. Wyck, dressed in his shorts and tank, nods once at me over Griffin's shoulder. From the mischievous grin on his face, I'll bet he's remembering our last meeting. Griffin releases me and looks around. "Wow! An obstacle course! I never get to do anything as cool as this!"

"Yeah, well, it's not as much fun as it looks. Have you two been waiting outside this whole time?"

"Pretty much," Griffin replies. "Commander Matthews told us to wait until he finished assessing you then I'm supposed to show you what I can do."

Before I can reply, Carter walks in. He's carrying his own tablet. Without saying a word, he begins tapping on Lewis's tablet. With a shake of his head, he asks, "Lewis, what did you do?" Then he calls out, "Commander, this will take a little time."

"Very well. Lewis, notify me when the course is ready. I will be in my office until then. Griffin, perhaps now would be a good time for you to show Vivian what you can do," Hoyt announces from his vantage point above us, and because of that strange connection between us, I feel him leaving.

"Yes, sir!" Griffin's face is all excited-puppy smiles again.

Wyck wheels over a dummy that has been standing at the back of the room before stepping clear. "There you go, Griff."

"Thanks, Wyck. Okay, Vivian, you do something to the dummy, and I'll reverse it," he explains.

"Alright, but if you reverse it, how will I remember doing anything in the first place?"

"You'll remember because you're Gifted. Regular people don't remember. They never realize anything has happened, but if you have some power, you will remember. That's how I know Wyck is Gifted, too. He can remember the before and after." Griffin clamps his brother lovingly on the back. "It's just a matter of time, right Wyck?"

Wyck shakes his head. "I'm not holding my breath. I've told you a million times. It's probably just because we're twins."

"No, it's not. Commander Matthews says we have to be patient. It will happen." He positions himself behind me. "I'm ready when you are, Vivian."

Shrugging, I say, "Here goes." And I let loose a small blast, enough to blacken the dummy's chest but not enough to destroy it.

Before I can turn around to give Griffin the go ahead, the unmarked dummy stares back at me.

"Whoa, that's pretty cool," I say over my shoulder.

"Wanna do it again?" he asks.

"Sure." And for the next half hour, we destroy and repair the dummy over and over. While we're practicing, Wyck has moved to the punching bag where he's kicking and punching like a rehearsed dance routine.

Griffin sits down on the mat while I retrieve two bottles of water from a fridge built into the wall. "Sorry, I need a break. It takes a lot out of me to reverse that many times."

"No problem. I could use a break, too." I unscrew the cap from my bottle and take a sip. Wyck catches my eye and motions me over to him. I pass Carter who is still grumbling at an upset Lewis. When I reach the punching bag, Wyck grabs my water and takes a long swig. He hands it back, but I shake my head.

"Keep it," I say, curling up my lip.

He smiles. "Scared I got germs, princess? After that kiss the other night, I wouldn't think you'd be worried about sharing my germs." He laughs and drinks again.

"Don't say that!" I exclaim a little too loudly and draw Lewis's curious stare. I whisper, "That wasn't real. Besides, that was your fantasy, not mine." I try to be angry, but I can't stop the smile I try to hide.

"Keep tellin' yourself that, princess." He pulls me closer. "I know how we can get those codes we need to unlock the files." I follow the slight tilt of his chin toward Carter. "If anyone knows, Carter will. You just have to pull them out of his brain."

"Oh, is that all? Sure, Wyck, I'll get right on that." I roll my eyes. "You think it's that easy? Walk up and yank them out, here, in front of Griffin and Lewis?"

"No, smart ass, I don't. We have to find a way for you to talk to him alone. Maybe you could tell him you need to be cleared for access into the training center so you can practice whenever you want." He looks pleased with his suggestion.

"Not gonna happen. Matthews will have told him not to do that. Any other ideas, *smart ass*?"

He watches Carter who is speaking into his wrist radio. "Tell him you want him to build you a device, something that will help you enhance your abilities."

"Enhance my abilities? Like a lightning rod?" I snort, imagining myself in an aluminum helmet with a three-foot spike on top.

"How about something to help your aim?" He smirks as he turns the punching bag around to show me a charred star pattern on the side.

I watch Carter while the arrogant pygmy yells at Lewis. I could flatter him, make him think it's his idea. It might work. We would be close enough for me to snatch his memories, and if I don't manage to get what I need, the device will give me an excuse to speak to him again.

Wyck eyes me closely. "You know it will work. You can thank me later." His arm brushes mine as he walks away.

"In your dreams." I'm annoyed at myself for noticing how his shorts fit him in all the right places.

He turns around, walking backward. "I hope so, princess," he says with that signature cocky smile. Wyck leaves, clapping Carter on the shoulder as he passes him. Carter, nonplussed by the familiar gestures, looks as though someone has just spit on him, but Wyck doesn't notice or doesn't care and keeps walking right out the door.

"Where's he going?" Griffin asks from beside me.

"I don't know. I guess he was tired." I hope he hasn't been standing there long enough to notice how closely I've been watching his brother. I need to get away from Wyck as soon as possible. Something about him unsettles me. I don't like how much he distracts me.

"I'm going to check on him. He's been so depressed lately. See you later, Vivian." Griffin jogs after Wyck.

I approach Carter as speaks into his radio. "I don't know, Commander. The whole system has shut down. There must be a mechanical failure. I'll have to dismantle the control box to check the connections." He presses his earpiece then replies, "Yes, sir. I'll tell Lewis. Lewis, Commander Matthews wants you to take One to eat then back to her room," Carter says in Lewis's general directions since he hasn't taken his eyes from his tablet's screen.

"Yes, sir. Come on, One." He motions me toward the door.

Before I can figure out how to get rid of Lewis so that I can brain-jack Carter, Ferguson runs into the room.

"Where is Commander Matthews?" he asks breathlessly. His excited voice draws Carter's attention away from the tablet.

"He's in his office. Why didn't you radio him?" Carter asks.

"This is not something he wants discussed over the radio," Ferguson replies, giving Carter a very pointed look as though they share a secret.

"Oh! Is it the Fire Element?" Carter grabs up both tablets when Ferguson nods and starts to leave the room.

"Wait!" I yell. "I need to talk to you, sir." I reach out and touch his arm. He flinches and pulls his arm away. "Please, it's important." I nearly throw up in my mouth from having to be nice to him.

"Ferguson, wait for me outside." Ferguson snarls at me as he walks away.

"Lewis, I really want to speak with Mr. Carter alone." I take a chance and connect with Lewis's mind. He nods and walks out behind Ferguson.

"What is it, One? I don't have all day," he snaps.

"Well, after practice today, I think I need some help and you're the only one smart enough to help." I smile shyly at him.

He raises an eyebrow. "What do you need from me?"

"I want something to help me focus my power more, something to improve my aim." I sit down in the chair to make him feel taller while I smile again.

"Hm… something to fit your palm and direct the beam more precisely?" He takes my hand and turns it over. I force myself not to yank it away.

"Exactly! I knew you would understand!" He runs his finger down my palm.

"Yes, well, I'll talk to the commander about it—"

"No!" His eyes grow large at my outburst. "I think we should keep it between the two of us until it's finished. I want to surprise Commander Matthews, show him that I'm committed to the cause. I know that I haven't been exactly eager, but I want to change that." Nodding, I touch his arm flirtatiously. "I would be very grateful."

His smile reminds me of a lizard, and my skin crawls. "Fine, I'll keep it a secret, and I'll contact you when it's ready to be fitted." He turns to leave, but I grab him.

"One more thing," I say, staring hard into his eyes and willing him to let me in. Carter's mind is like Fort Knox. I search as quickly as possible and manage to pry some computer codes from his brain.

I have no way of knowing if they're the right ones or not. I'm scared to stay longer. Carter's too intelligent, and I'm afraid his brain will rebel. I release him, and he staggers slightly.

"You okay? You should sit down," I say guiding him to the chair.

"What...," he begins but grabs his head.

"You said your head hurt then I thought you were going to pass out. You really should take better care of yourself, Mr. Carter. This place could never run without you." I touch his shoulder. "I'm sure Commander Matthews wouldn't mind if you went to lie down." My statement has just the effect I expect. Carter leaps to his feet.

"Go with Lewis to your room, One. I'll call for you when I have a chance." He rushes toward the door.

* * *

A couple of hours later I'm nearly asleep when Wallis comes in without bothering to knock.

"Get up, Vivian. We have to go!" He tosses my boots at the bed.

"What? What's going on?" I sit up and begin tugging them on. "Is it Easton? Oh no, it's Abby, isn't it? She's worse!" I hurriedly tie them and slap my hair into a ponytail.

"No, we have a mission. We have to move fast! Come on!" He grabs my arm a little too tightly and pulls me to my feet.

"A mission?! What does that mean?" I jerk my arm from his hand.

"We're going after someone—a Fire Element. You've been commanded to go." He yanks again, but I stand my ground. "Vivian, don't be difficult. You're just making this harder than it has to be."

"No! I won't go! I refuse to go 'after' another person!" I yell, arms akimbo.

"I didn't want to do this." He pulls his gun out and speaks into his wrist radio. "Lewis, bring Abby."

"No! No, leave her alone! I'll go; just keep her here and safe!" My temper flares at being powerless, and I shove my glowing hand behind me.

He radios Lewis. "Stand down, Lewis."

Wallis holsters his gun. "I'm sorry, Vivian, but you left me no choice. It's my job to get you there, no matter what I have to do."

Even while I'm glaring at him, I know that it's not really his fault. We're all pawns in Hoyt's game. Wallis might think he's chosen this righteous path, but he couldn't get out if he wanted to.

I follow blindly until he doesn't turn in the direction I expect him to turn. According to the mental map I stole from Wallis when I was searching for the surveillance room, we aren't going to the main entrance where Easton and I were brought that first day.

"Wallis, where are we going? And why are you walking so fast?" I'm practically jogging to keep up with him. We turn again, and I realize we aren't far from the prisoners' quarters.

"We're taking an exit on the far side of the facility. We'll be flying to our destination," he says.

"Wallis, please let me go see Easton. We're really close, and I'll hurry." Wallis doesn't know that I'm going to see Easton, one way or another.

"We don't have time, Vivian." He continues walking, but he stops when he realizes I'm not with him.

"I promise to do whatever you tell me to do for the rest of the day, but I *am* going to see him." Just when I think I'm going to have to mentally coerce him, he sighs and throws up his hands. He starts down the hallway toward the cells.

"Five minutes" He opens the hidden door. "I'll wait here."

"Thank you. I'll be fast." I'm already jogging toward his cell. A quick glance shows me that Abby and Cooper still aren't in their cell.

Easton is waiting for me at the bars of the cell, but one glimpse of his face tells me he hasn't forgotten our fight. He doesn't reach for me, but I take his hand through the bars. "I'm sorry. I didn't mean to upset you the last time I was here." He holds my eyes with his intense blue-green gaze. "Are you still angry with me? Say something, please."

He pulls his hand away and steps back. "I saw you, Vivian. I saw you with him." He grits his teeth and clenches his jaw. "You and him" —he takes a breath and closes his eyes— "kissing."

Shit! He saw Wyck and me in the closet, and even though it wasn't real, it would seem like it in his head. How will I ever convince him that I didn't kiss Wyck?

"No, Easton, you don't understand." I grab the bars.

He shakes his head and snorts grimly. "You're right. I don't. Make me understand. Make me understand how you could do that."

"But I wasn't. I didn't do anything! What you saw wasn't real!" I put my forehead against the bars. "It was a... a fantasy." But as soon as I say it, I know I've screwed up.

He raises his brows and casts his eyes to the ceiling. "A fantasy? A fantasy of you and another guy! Oh that makes it all clear, Vivian!"

"Not my fantasy! It was Wyck. It popped in my head from his, and you must have seen it. It wasn't real. I would never do that to you!" But guilt threatens to choke me because I'm affected by Wyck's thoughts—and by Wyck—even if I don't want to be.

"Wyck? That's his name?" Suddenly, Easton lunges toward the bars, forcing a tiny squeal from me. "Is he a freak like the rest of them?" His face blanches, and I know he didn't mean it the way it came out, but it still hurts.

"You mean like me?"

"Vivian, I didn't mean—" he begins, but I stop him.

My eyes fill, and a tear slips out and tracks down my cheek. "No, Easton, at least right now he's a normal guy, and he's helping me figure out a way to get all of us out of here. I have to leave. I'm going on some kind of mission tonight. I asked Wallis to let me talk to you, to apologize." I try to pull my hands from the bars, but he grabs my wrist. He touches my face, his eyes searching and holding mine. I open my mind, hoping he can see the truth even if it means showing him the way Wyck sometimes makes me feel. He pulls my face close to his and rests his forehead against mine. I hear his thoughts.

I love you, Vivian.

I cry harder when I hear his simple statement and know it's true. "I love you, too, Easton."

"Come back safely to me." He kisses me softly.

I try to tell him I will, but the words stick in my throat.

CHAPTER THIRTY-TWO

I'VE NEVER FLOWN BEFORE NOW, but even I can tell this is not a standard, government-issue plane. Though it's not large, it seats five of us comfortably and could accommodate several more. From the soft, leather seats to the individual work spaces, this thing epitomizes luxury.

Wallis, Lilah, Wyck, Griffin, and I have been in the air for a couple of hours, flying through the night sky. Lilah has her eyes closed but is listening to some 'screamo' band so loudly that I doubt she's sleeping. Griffin's overflowing excitement causes him to talk nonstop, and it grates on my frayed nerves. Wyck, who has long since given up paying attention to him, has moved to the seat next to me to let Wallis deal with his rambling.

Several times Wyck has initiated conversations, but my fight with Easton keeps flashing through my mind like one of those huge lane-closed signs on the interstate, reminding me of how dangerous a friendship with him could be. Even if I never allow anything to happen between the two of us, simply being near him has already caused a divide with Easton. Besides, I can't focus on much at the moment anyway. My mind is reeling with what I'm about to do.

"So where's the commander?" Griffin asks Wallis as Wallis shuffles a deck of cards and hands them to Griffin. In an attempt to distract Griffin, Wallis suggested a game of solitaire.

"He's already there. He left as soon as Ferguson and Carter gave him the news."

"What exactly are we doing, Wallis?" Wyck asks from the seat to my right.

Wallis sighs. "I don't suppose it will hurt to brief you now since we're already in route. The commander said to wait till we were in the van, but I don't see why it would hurt to do it now." Even Lilah perks up and pulls out her ear buds, confirming my suspicion that she hadn't been asleep at all.

"Our mission is to secure an adolescent male Element. He's been under surveillance for some time, and today, the opportunity we've been waiting for presented itself," Wallis explains.

"What's his property?" Lilah asks, stretching her arms above her head before flinging her skinny jean-clad legs sideways across her seat. "You know how I hate surprises, Wally." She glances pointedly at me.

"Fire, and don't call me that, the first we've had in a very long time. Commander Matthews wants this one badly." His eyes lock on mine. "Failure is *not* an option."

"I'm guessing since we're all going, this boy isn't too excited about joining," Wyck says, moving toward the mini-fridge under a counter at the back of the cabin.

"No, but he'll come around." Wallis shrugs. "Everyone does eventually."

"So why am I here? I can't do anything." Wyck reaches inside for a can of soda.

"Ah, Wyck, maybe today will be the day when our wittle man will grow into a big boy like his big brother, Griffin," Lilah sneers. "Oh, I wish I had my camera." She flutters her hands and pretends to wipe away a tear.

"You'll be the first to know, Aunty Lilah." Wyck raises his soda in a mock toast. "Here's to hoping it's something nasty and potentially painful."

"Commander Matthews wants you here. That's all that's important." Wallis swings around to look at Lilah. "And you be nice."

"I want you here, too," Griffin, who's been surprisingly quiet, says. "You help keep me from being so nervous."

"This is you not nervous?" Lilah snorts. "You haven't shut up since we left. Remind me to bring a muzzle next time." She starts to cram her ear buds back into her ears.

From his place leaning against the counter, Wyck shakes his head. "Have you always been a bitch, or is this a recent development?"

I can't stop my hoot of laughter and continue chuckling even when she glares at me across the plane before turning her evil eye on Wyck.

"Pretty ballsy, Wyck, for somebody whose only weapon is that asshole smile. It might work on this one"—she points at me with her black finger-nailed hand—"but I won't hesitate to make you think we're on the ground and watch you walk out that door in midair." She throws up her hands. "Better yet, I'll make you think bubby here"— she nods at Griffin—"is the big, bad terrorist who killed daddy and let you kill him then you'll kill yourself and end all our misery!"

At the mention of terrorists, Griffin sucks in a breath, and for the first time since meeting him, I see rage in his navy eyes. Before any of us can stop him, Griffin launches himself at Lilah, pulls a knife from his Batman-style utility belt, and plunges it into Lilah's chest.

"Griffin!" Wyck screams, grabbing for him. Wallis leaps to his feet.

Lilah's kohl-rimmed eyes widen when she yanks at the knife. She's grappling with the bloody blade when her eyes slide closed, the crimson darkening the yellow of her t-shirt.

"Fix it!" Wyck yells, staring in horror at his seemingly angelic brother.

Griffin, smiling chillingly, says, "Of course, Wyck." Then, quick as a flash, everyone has returned to his or her pre-slasher positions. Wyck's leaning against the counter, breathing heavily. Griffin is still sickly beaming, but Lilah's smugness has vanished along with the knife and the blood. She grabs her chest as though the knife remains.

Nostrils flaring, her voice shakes with fury. "When I finish with you, you'll be begging for death!" She closes her eyes, and the plane's interior begins to fade, but before she can complete her vision, Wallis steps between Griffin and Lilah.

"Enough! We're landing in fifteen minutes! We don't have time for these games! Griffin, go sit near the front, and don't so much as look at her!"

We're once again inside the opulent plane, and Lilah is angrily shoving her ear buds into her ears while Griffin brushes past her to sit with Wallis. As he sits, Wallis sits, and without looking at him, says in a low voice, "Commander Matthews expects more from you than childish parlor tricks."

Griffin nods ashamedly and drops his head. "Should I apologize?" Griffin asks, behaving again like his usual friendly self.

"Not unless you want to die." Wallis shakes his head and smiles. "Kid, first thing you need to learn about females is never, never apologize immediately when they think you've messed up—or in this case, when you've stabbed her in the chest. She won't believe you're sincere anyway and"—he draws his finger across his throat in a cutting motion—"it puts you in striking distance." Griffin nods, and Wallis pats his shoulder fatherly.

As I start to smile at Wallis's advice, realization of what he just said jerks me up straighter in my seat. He told Griffin not to apologize too fast 'when you've stabbed her in the chest.' How could he know that? In the training center, Griffin said only the Gifted can tell time had been altered. That could only mean Wallis has a power! He's been lying to me this entire time! Granted, I never really *asked* him if he had a power; I'd only assumed, but still! I like Wallis, have actually felt bad about giving him trouble. He'd said I was like his annoying little sister. We'd bonded over jello! How could I be so wrong about someone I liked so much? Wait! That's it! Wallis is a Magnet. He has to be. That would explain why I like him so much!

Disappointment twists my heart. He doesn't really like me, and my friendly attachments are as fake as Trista Parmer's boobs. They put him with me, just like Mr. Lewis. This is their game board. I'm only one more piece to manipulate so they can win, and here I am about to do the same thing to some other kid.

When the plane begins its descent, I remember that between my Easton drama and the fatal stabbing, I still haven't told Wyck the codes I stole from Carter's brain. The pilot's voice announces his preparation to land as I close my eyes and search for Wyck's mind connection.

Wyck, nod if you can hear me.

When he nods slowly once, I continue, pouring in numbers and letter combos.

Hope you can remember all this.

But even as I say it, he's pulling out a small notepad and pencil from the workspace before him.

Is that smart? Writing it down?

He rolls his eyes but continues writing.

No one but Carter would understand it, princess, and I'm putting this some place nobody's gonna search.

He tears the page loose and shoves it into the front of his pants. I whip my head away, embarrassment reddening my ears, but as I do, the scene from the closet flashes into my mind. I'd like to blame him, but the truth is clear when he grins and leans in next to me.

"On second thought, maybe I was wrong about that." He laughs loudly enough to catch Griffin's notice, but the 'fasten seat belts' light comes on before Griffin can ask why my cheeks are blazing.

* * *

The dawn can't be far away. We've been waiting for what feels like forever in this van in front of a large, institutional-like compound called Highest Point Rehabilitation Center, waiting for orders. Judging by the razor wire and barred windows, my guess is this is not a place you want to be for any length of time. My stomach growls noisily.

"Eat this." Leaning between the driver and passenger seats, Wallis shoves a candy bar into my hands.

"I'm fine," I say even as my stomach rumbles at the thought of chocolate and peanuts. I don't want anything from Wallis, not now that I know what a fraud his kindness is.

"Eat the damn thing." Lilah grabs it from him, throwing it at my head from where she sits next to me. "Your stomach's louder than their whispering." She jerks her thumb over her shoulder toward the twins where they sit in the back seat.

For the last few minutes the twins have had their heads together, whispering heatedly. At Lilah's comment, Wyck flips her the bird. "Bite me, freak," he says.

"Like I haven't heard *that* before. Real original, loser. Hell, my druggie mom had better names than that!" She leans over the seat to glare at him.

"Shut up, both of you!" Ferguson yells from the driver's seat. He traveled with Hoyt and arrived earlier than us, meeting us at the small, rural airport. "Wallis, go see what the holdup is," he orders.

"He'll let us know if he needs us." Wallis grits his teeth. When Ferguson pulled up in the van, Wallis had mumbled something under his breath before climbing inside. This waiting game has been none too pleasant for him either.

"So what's this kid's name?" Lilah asks, yawning loudly and breaking off half of the candy bar I just opened.

"That's need to know, Lilah. Right now, you don't need to know." Wallis doesn't bother looking at her.

But Lilah, undaunted and chewing open-mouthed, redirects her question to Ferguson. "So, Fergie, what's this kid's name?"

Turning sideways, I look at Wyck and smother my laughter. If only the two of us didn't know why she called him that!

"Fergie? 'Real original', Lilah." Wyck snorts, not bothering to hide his amusement.

Ferguson responds without turning around. "Zebidiah something."

"Is this a prison or what?" Lilah continues.

"It's a maximum security, government facility for criminal deviants," Wallis says as though he's reading from a cue card.

"What does that mean?" Griffin asks.

"It's a place where they send some of the worst criminals, sick psychos," Ferguson answers.

"Oh, perfect place for you, Lilah. How do we sign her up?" Wyck asks.

She ignores him. "What the hell did he do to get sent here? Even I didn't end up in a place like this." She looks out at the pre-dawn landscape. "It's practically in the middle of the desert."

"What he did isn't important. Our job is to take him from here." Wallis rubs his forehead.

Ferguson shakes his head at Wallis. "He burned down his house with his entire family inside. We assume he manifested the fire, but we aren't sure if it was intentional or not."

"He killed his whole family? And we want him to join us?" I ask.

"Why not? We got you didn't we? I mean what you've done is sort of the same thing, isn't it Vivian?" Lilah smirks with that same half-smile that seems permanently affixed to her smug face.

The tension in the car is palpable. Immediate silence descends. Like her comment about the twins' parents earlier, this one's hitting below the belt. It's low even for her. My chest tingles. I breathe deeply and close my eyes. My brain refuses to let her bait me again, but my body feels otherwise. One tiny zap can't hurt anything, right? When I open my eyes, her face is bathed in gray-white light. I distantly hear Wallis trying to stop me and Ferguson yelling something about his Taser, but nothing they say matters at this moment. "You don't get it, do you, Lilah? I've been to hell and back. I'm not afraid of anything you can do to me."

"Really? You seemed scared enough that night in your dream when you thought your boyfriend was gonna die. You know, I've been thinking," she says tilting her head thoughtfully. "I might pay him a visit, let him know about the 'come screw me' looks between you and Wyck. Maybe—What's his name? Easton?—will think differently about his incarceration, or maybe I'll show up looking like you and see how that goes." She raises her brows. "Could be fun." She leers at me.

"Get out of the van, Lilah." I'm so angry by this point that I can't fight it.

"You gonna make me?"

"Get out of the van, Lilah," I repeat.

"But I can't." She closes her eyes. Immediately, the scene changes, and Lilah, Wallis, Ferguson, and the twins vanish. I'm still inside a van, but it's a prisoner transport van like the one used to bring Easton and me to the mountain—except, this isn't *that* van.

This van is turned on its side. Glass fragments litter the floor, and Aunt Charlotte lies among them, pink pajamas stained scarlet from the shard protruding from her chest. Even though my brain knows this isn't real, my eyes fill with tears, and my stomach lurches into my throat. I don't know how Lilah knows, but it's almost exactly like that night.

"I can't get out, Vivian," Aunt Charlotte's image says, blood oozing from the corner of her mouth. She begins to sob. "I'm not ready to die!"

This isn't real. This isn't real. This isn't...

"I know," I whisper. "I'm sorry."

"You did this! I wouldn't be here if I hadn't taken you in! If you had stayed home and protected me instead of going to prom, I wouldn't have been taken! It's your fault, Vivian!" She sits up; blood pours from her chest toward my knees where I'm kneeling beside her. Her face contorts into an evil mask, eyes flashing hatred. "You're nothing but a freak!"

"No!" I yell. I'm light-headed; my vision is going dark. As I'm about to spin into the darkness, I'm jerked backward. Someone is gently patting my cheeks, speaking softly. "Vivian, come back to me. Vivian."

My eyelids are heavy, but I force them open. Wallis's face is above me, and he smiles. "Good, good, Vivian. It wasn't real. It's okay." He helps me sit and offers me water from a bottle in his hand.

When I put my hand down to steady myself, I feel the grit of sand. Looking around, I see the sun peeking over the horizon, already heating the desert air.

Then I remember. I remember why I'm sitting on the ground between a dirt road and scrubby cactus. I remember why I can hear Lilah's cackling through the open van door and see her bent double with laughter at my expense.

Fury blinds me. I yank up my hand.

"Vivian, no!" Wallis yells, grabbing for my hand. He jumps in front of me. "Stop! We are all on the same team. Don't do this now!"

"Move, Wallis." My voice shakes with restraint as Wallis's face and body turn into giant, pulsing bull's-eyes.

He reaches up and touches his ear. "Roger that," he says into his wrist radio. "Let's go." He begins to pull me away by the hand but turns back. "Just, Vivian."

Lilah leans out the still-open door; laughter gone, she's now puffed up like a toad frog at being slighted. "He didn't ask for me? You heard wrong, Wallis. I'm sure he needs me," she replies, stepping out.

"Lilah, get back in the van," Wallis orders. "You've been a pain in the ass, and when he hears about what you did, he's not going to be pleased. Get back in the van!"

Forgetting he's supposed to be restraining me from firing on Lilah, Wallis releases my wrist and points at her. Quick as lightning, I lift my hand.

"Let me help you." I let loose a blast strong enough to slam her back inside. Her head shatters the tinted glass of the door window on the other side, and she slides unconscious to the van floor. "Oops, guess that was a teeny-weeny bit too hard." I shrug, smile sweetly, and walk toward the entrance, a stunned Wallis in my wake.

By the time I reach the double doors, he's caught up and is holding a door open for me. I pause in front of him. Even if I feel betrayed by him, I can't ignore that he helped me out by pulling me from that vision. "Thank you for waking me. I know I'm only an assignment for you, but I do appreciate it."

"You're not just an 'assignment,' not anymore. I see you as my friend. Don't you see me as your friend?" he asks as he awkwardly pats my shoulder like he's not sure if I'm going to kill him.

"When this is over, we need to talk before I can answer that."

"Fair enough," he says, pressing his earpiece again. "Let's move. Commander Matthews needs you."

Every doorway is barred, and guards must unlock each set of doors. At last we arrive in what I assume is the mess hall by the number of tables. A couple of the tabletops are smoking and charred. Fire extinguisher residue covers one table, and the slight smoke makes me sneeze.

Hoyt's positioned near the entrance, and across the expansive room, a small boy stands in prison-orange scrubs. Even from this distance I can see the fear on his face. This is the fire starter? He's a scared kid who can't be more than thirteen and probably weighs less than I do.

"You rang, master." I scowl at Hoyt, but he smiles.

"Well, at last you understand your place, my dear." He turns toward the boy. "Let me introduce you to Zebidiah, who insists on being called Zeb" —he wrinkles his nose in disgust—"though the reason escapes me. He is a tad reluctant to join us, Vivian. It is your task to convince him otherwise." Hoyt's expression is firm, his black marble eyes making him appear fierce regardless of his mood.

"By 'convince' you mean threaten?" I ask, glancing back at his tiny frame.

"No, I mean force. There is a van waiting to take him. Put him in it."

"Too much for you, Hoyt? Can't you handle a boy? You must be slipping." I shake my head in mock sympathy.

"I do not have time for this banter, Vivian. You and I have another small task after this one." He speaks into his radio. "Ferguson, call Lewis. Tell him to ready the girl."

I don't have to ask. He means Abby. "Fine. Any suggestions?" I snarl my lip. You've obviously been at this a while already." I gesture around.

"You are a Water and Energy Element. Use either. Use both." He throws up both hands. I think he might actually be frustrated. "I do not care, but be successful. Your friend's depending on it." He moves behind me, motioning for Wallis to do the same.

Now what? Pretend he's Lilah and blast him through the wall? I'll try reason first.

"Hey, Zeb, I'm Vivian." I begin walking slowly toward him.

He steps back against the wall. "Don't come any closer!" His pubescent voice cracks. "I... I don't want to hurt you, but I will!" He holds out his hand, palm up. Immediately, a tiny flame jumps to life, like he's holding an invisible lighter. The flame grows, burning blue at the base.

"Listen, I know how you feel. I didn't want to go with this guy either." I motion backward with my head "But it's got to be better than this place! Come on, the uniforms are way cooler," I say, smiling and hoping I can charm him. But he's not interested because he turns his hand palm out, and flames shoot forward several feet, nearly reaching me.

"Whoa! I'll be honest, Zeb. If I don't get you in the van outside, this douche bag is going to kill my best friend. You don't want that, do you?" When he shoots another jet at me, I decide reasoning time is over. "Guess you do. Alright then, can't say I didn't warn you."

When I raise my glowing palm, he blasts me with fire. I barely have time to throw out an energy shield and block the heat before he fires again, and this time he doesn't stop. A continuous stream of flames surrounds my energy orb. Even inside its protection, the heat intensifies. I've got to douse this kid's flame. Time to test this water theory.

Above me, exposed pipes run the length of the room. Scattered along its length are sprinklers. I have no idea how to make this work, so I select the closest one to Zeb and concentrate. Nothing happens.

I can't fail. I think of Abby, her blonde curls, her purple glasses. She was so scared and sick when I saw her last. All of a sudden, water begins to drip from the sprinkler. How did I do that? I have to do it again. Okay, think about Abby. A collage of images assault me—Abby in her car, Abby in her prom dress last spring, Abby in shock over touching a fish. The drip becomes a trickle. Zeb is too busy blasting me to notice the puddle forming near him.

Thinking of all those good times with Abby has made me feel... happy, and feeling happy makes me think of Easton, his dark hair, his lopsided grin, his lips on mine. With a rushing sound, water gushes from the sprinkler, breaking off the round head. The force doesn't stop. The pipe above begins to crack, and water surges onto Zeb. The key to controlling the water is emotion. Didn't Hoyt mention something like that when he told me about it?

The flames stop as the water pours down. Zeb's high-pitch screams echo around the room.

"Had enough, Zeb?" He sputters and falls to the hard floor. "What's that? I can't hear you, buddy?" I stop the flow, throw an energy orb through the only window to break out the bars and metal screen, and wrap Zeb in a rope of power like I did Lilah in the training center. I'm not taking any chances with this kid.

"Tell the men to pull the van around, Wallis." I hide my shock when he jumps into action and does it. When the men park the van beside the wall and open the back, I lift Zeb and put him inside, allowing them the chance to shackle him before I release him.

Hoyt looks pleased. "Well done, my dear. Wallis, you will accompany Vivian and me on a short journey. Tell Ferguson to take the others back to the facility." Hoyt walks briskly through the doors.

"Yes, Commander." Wallis gives me a quick thumbs up sign before radioing Ferguson and giving him his order.

"Where are we going?" I ask when Wallis finishes and motions me through the way we entered.

"I don't know, but he rarely takes only one other of the Gifted with him," Wallis says with an excited smile.

"You mean two, don't you?" I don't look at him, but I feel his wince.

"So, you know. Who told you?" He leads me through door after door.

"You told on yourself today when you were talking to Griffin. You remembered the time change." We walk to a limo parked close by. Before he opens the door, I stop him. "What I don't get is if you're a Magnet, why didn't they just use you instead of bringing in Mr. Lewis? It's the same power, right?"

"Yes, it's the same, but Mr. Lewis could draw multiple people at the same time. His age made him powerful. For what it's worth, Vivian, I meant it when I said you aren't just an assignment, and I haven't used my power on you in days." He opens the back door and smiles. "So, uh, don't kill me, okay?"

"Wallis, have I killed anyone today? Why would I start with you?"

CHAPTER THIRTY-THREE

THE BLUE-GREEN OCEAN reminds me of Easton. I've never actually seen the ocean, so today's been a day of firsts for me.

After leaving the prison, we were driven back to the airport where we boarded a plane as nice as the one that brought us to the prison then we drove to this beautiful stretch of white sand and palm trees. For the last twenty minutes I've shivered in a pair of running shorts and a sports bra, waiting for a man I don't know. At first, I pretended to jog like Hoyt told me to while he and Wallis hide in the lifeguard stand I'm leaning against.

I was briefed on my mission in the car. I'm supposed to blend in (on an empty beach, BTW) until a blond man shows up to swim. After he begins his routine swim out to the buoy, Hoyt will emerge from his hiding place and tell me what to do next.

I'm beginning to think my 'mark' won't show when whistling catches my attention. A tall man with honey-blond hair walks briskly from the direction of the parking area. With his blue swim trunks and muscular build, he looks like an ad for suntan lotion or surfboards. I put one leg on the lifeguard stand and stretch. He nods and smiles before tossing his towel on the beach and jumping into the water.

As soon as he's under, Hoyt joins me. "Are you ready, my dear?" he asks excitedly.

"Ready for what?" I drop the pretense of stretching and watch the golden god as he cuts through the water.

"To give this man a poetic last moment. Control the current; create a strong undertow. I will do the rest." He puts up his hands and a gentle breeze begins to blow.

"But won't that pull him out to sea?" I ask, beginning to see what I'm really about to do.

"Precisely," he says. The wind picks up, blowing the loose strands of hair around my face.

"We're going to kill him, aren't we?" My stomach churns.

"Yes, we are." He states it so matter-of-factly that I stare at him. At this point, nothing he does should surprise me, but as the full force of his declaration sinks in, my knees go weak, and I'm forced to support myself against the lifeguard stand.

"Why? What's he done?" I'm hoping he'll say this man is a murderer, a serial killer who targets old women and their kittens.

"He angered the wrong people. He's a foreign diplomat, Vivian, and his politics aren't... acceptable. He has a fondness for early-morning swims in the ocean, thinks a pool is too ordinary, as luck would have it." He smiles viciously. "Lucky for us, that is. This is what we do. We resolve sticky situations."

"I can't. I won't do it," I say, watching the man turn and start out again.

"Oh, Vivian, you make me tired. Must we go through all this again? Poor Abby needs her rest. She doesn't need Lewis waking her because you keep forgetting your role in this organization." He sighs, drops his hands, and pulls a phone from his pocket.

While I watch him click it on, I know I have no choice. I'm going to have to kill this man—a man whose crime is his political view.

"Lewis," Hoyt says into the phone.

"Okay," I whisper.

"Standby, Lewis. No, do not wake her yet. I will have Wallis notify you when we are finished." He disconnects and slips the phone back into his pocket.

He raises his hands again. "Begin, Vivian."

I concentrate like I did earlier in the facility mess hall with Zeb. Abby, Cooper, Easton, Aunt Charlotte—they all dance through my mind. I try to focus on the good memories, but this time, I feel only the sadness and fear. But that's enough. The man begins to struggle against the wind and water.

"Wonderful." Hoyt almost chuckles.

In only a minute, the man with the gilded hair goes under. He fights and calls for help, but we're the only people on the beach. As he goes under for the final time, I sink to my knees and throw up in the sand. How will I ever live with this? How will I ever sleep again without seeing his face?

"Don't worry, my dear. You will sleep again eventually, and until then, the staff doctor will make you sleep." Hoyt hauls me roughly to my feet.

"Stay out of my head, you bastard!" I try to tug my arm from his grasp, but he pulls me closer.

"You will not brood on this. It will make you weak, and I won't allow it. If I must, I will invade your brain and yank out every thought in your head! Do you understand?" He's so close that I see myself reflected in his eyes.

"If you could do that, you already would have. Now let me go!" When I wrench away this time, he releases me, and I walk toward the car, wishing I were the golden man.

CHAPTER THIRTY-FOUR

"I DIDN'T GET IT ALL." Wyck plops down in the armchair and rubs his forehead. "I got a lot but not everything."

I've been lying in bed since we returned yesterday morning even though my door is no longer locked. I guess Hoyt thinks I've proven my loyalty with that sick initiation on the beach. As soon as we returned, I showered, put on my pajamas, and climbed into bed. Wallis has brought food a few times, but I can't bring myself to touch it. A tray of cold food is sitting on the table near the door.

I asked Wallis to let Easton know I'd returned safely but not to mention what I'd done. I don't know how I'll ever tell him I helped kill a man. He'll assure me that I had no choice, that I did it to save Abby, but that's not enough.

"Are you listening?" Wyck leans forward and waves his hand. "Hello, Earth to Vivian."

Giving my head a shake, I sit up against some pillows, pull my hair into a bun, and try to pay attention. "Sorry, Wyck."

"What's up with you today, anyway? And why haven't I seen you in the mess hall? Are you sick?" He picks at a perfectly-placed rip in his designer jeans.

A part of me wants to tell Wyck what happened. Maybe if I let it out, it won't hurt so much, but I don't even know if I'm supposed to tell. "Nothing, go on and tell me what you found out."

He gives me that searching stare of his that always makes me feel like he's digging for secrets in my soul. "Alright" —he sighs— "who do you want to hear about first, yourself or Griffin and me?"

"You two. What did you find out?"

His expression turns serious as he leans forward, his elbows resting against his knees. "You were right. We can't trust good ole Commander Matthews. I think he killed my dad. From what I saw in our files, I think he orchestrated the attack that killed him. It probably wasn't terrorists at all."

I gasp. "Oh, Wyck, I'm so sorry." I crawl to the end of the bed near the armchair. "I know exactly what you're feeling."

"I can't say I'm all that surprised. I mean, you tried to tell me this place was bad, and I can tell he has no use for me since I have no power, but seeing it confirmed... Vivian, how will I tell Griffin? He's not going to believe it."

I hang my legs over the mattress and scoot close enough to touch his hand. "We'll figure it out. He has to be told. I'll tell him if you think it would help."

He looks up, his indigo eyes filled with fear. "It makes me worry about my mom. She was supposed to be there that day, you know. She was supposed to be at his office. They were going to have lunch together, but the car wouldn't start, so she canceled on him. She'd be dead, too." He laughs humorlessly before looking back at me again. "She could be dead right now, and we would never know it. They keep making excuses why we can't talk to her. They relay her messages, but we can never seem to get through to her when we call. It goes straight to voicemail. I have to know." He grips my hand tightly. "I have to get out of here and find out if she's still alive."

"Why would they hurt her now, Wyck? They already have you two." I ask, trying to reassure him even though I don't really believe it myself.

"Because *none* of you guys have parents. Lilah's mother overdosed, and she never knew her dad," he says, ticking off each of us on his fingers. "Your mom and your Aunt Charlotte are dead. Zeb's parents were killed in a house fire, and our dad died in that terrorist attack on his office building. Our mom is the only loose end."

The reality of what he's saying hits me like a bullet. He's absolutely right. Our parents were 'loose ends.' If they are gone, there's nothing stopping Hoyt.

"What about my dad?" I'm almost scared to hear the answer.

"Well... I... uh... I don't know how to say this exactly, so I'll just start at the beginning." He shifts uncomfortably in his chair then finally stands and begins pacing at the foot of the bed.

"Your file is more detailed than any of the other files. From what I can tell, they've traced your history, your family tree. Apparently, they've been watching you and your family a long time. It looks like for as long as the Liaisons have existed, they've known about your family. I'm not sure they haven't approached them before." He cracks his knuckles nervously. "There are a number of strange accidents in your file, including your grandmother, Veronica, who was killed in a bizarre car wreck."

"Wait, exactly how long has the group been around and stalking my family?"

"There are scans of a journal dating from around the mid-1700s, a man named St. Clair. He seems to have begun the journal as a record of a woman and her child who possessed power similar to yours but weaker. St. Clair was experimenting on an"—he motions with his hand, like he's trying to pull the word from midair—"elixir, or potion, to give himself eternal life, something about his 'beloved wife's death.' Anyway, he was scared of dying, so he was doing all these weird experiments, trying to find something that would make him live forever. Evidently, there was some accident in a storm involving this girl, Virginia, and her unborn child."

I interrupt, "Another 'v'—she has to be the origin of the energy property."

"Yeah, that's what I'm thinking, too. Anyhow, this St. Clair became obsessed with her, and after a year or so, he began searching for others with gifts. He used his money to convince them to work for him as a group of super spies. During the Revolutionary War, he played both sides, sold the secrets they'd gathered with their powers to the highest bidder and eliminated obstacles in any way he had to."

When he pauses, I think of the swimmer, see him going under, fighting for his life.

"Vivian"—Wyck snaps his fingers inches from my nose—"you're doing it again. What's wrong with you?"

"Nothing, sorry. Please don't stop. What did you find out about my father?" I ask again.

"I'm getting there. The records get sketchy after the journal. I guess the old man died," —he shrugs— "only a few notes here and there until Veronica, your grandmother. There's a newspaper article about the accident and an obituary mentioning her one living child, your mom Violet. With Violet, the records become more detailed again—health reports, grades, photos. I suppose they decided it was the right time to try again when she left home and enrolled in Harper's Grove Community College. She was away from her grandmother and Charlotte, and she was lonely. He stops pacing and sits down in front of me in the chair, reaching out to hold my hand as I'd done to him earlier. "So, they sent out an operative to... to... I don't know how to say this without upsetting you, Vivian."

"Just say it, Wyck!" Anxiety is making my heart pound so hard I can't believe he doesn't hear it.

"He was sent to seduce your mom, get her pregnant. He sat in her section at Smokey's Grill where she waitressed every day for two weeks, asked her out, and well, got her to fall in love with him. They thought that if she carried his child she would be likely to stay with him then he could convince her to join up, and they'd all live happily ever after."

He stops, but I can tell there's more he's holding back. "Keep going. I have to know everything." I squeeze his hand even though mine is sweaty and gross.

"You know already that your dad was Gifted. You inherited your water property and your healing from him, and from what I can tell, having two gifts is really unusual. I cross-referenced his file. I was only able to access part of it because his history stops after your mom."

"That's it then. He's dead, isn't he?" I ask, not entirely sure how I feel about it. If he played my mom for a fool, he deserved it, but if there's still a chance to see him...

"I don't know. It literally stops, no more mention of anything after her. But" —he exhales noisily— "that's not the important part."

" 'Not the important part!' What could be more important than finding out he was *ordered* to create me?"

He takes a deep breath. "Your dad's double gift wasn't chance. He was bred by the Liaisons, created as an experiment—their attempt to make the perfect weapon. They impregnated a female

Healer with the DNA from the two strongest males—a Water Element and an Air Element." He glances away. "Turns out she gave birth to twin boys. Both had healer properties, but the air and water properties didn't merge, so one became a Water Element, the other an Air Element."

When he finally locks eyes with me, I know what he's about to say as surely as if I've taken it from his mind.

"Your father, the Water Element, is named Harrison. His brother, the Air Element, is named Hoyt."

CHAPTER THIRTY-FIVE

HOYT'S MY UNCLE. Everything makes more sense—how he knew about my power, why we have this weird connection, what he's said about my father.

Wyck waits patiently in front of me while my brain tries to digest all of this. My father was genetically engineered by the Liaisons then sent out to seduce my mother in order to create me, their ultimate prize.

"Do you think he ever really cared about her?" I ask, though I know Wyck doesn't have the answer.

"I don't know, Vivian. It's strange that all his records stop after Violet. It's like he was erased from the group." He moves to sit beside me on the bed and puts his arm around me. "Maybe he did. Maybe he cared too much and couldn't go through with his mission in the end."

"I'd say he was pretty successful, Wyck." I motion to myself. "Hello, here I am."

"Not that part. Obviously, he was able to do that part. What I mean is maybe he couldn't betray her. Maybe he refused to convince her to join them." He sits quietly for a minute then his face lights up. "Maybe he did more than that. Maybe he helped her escape and went into hiding himself. That would explain why all mention of him stops."

I jump up and take his place pacing at the foot of the bed. "That's a romantic thought, but I'm not as optimistic as you are. My guess is they killed him."

"Vivian, if he were dead they would have recorded that." He huffs and shrugs. "They have records on your family that go back over two hundred years. If one of their agents was eliminated because of your mother, don't you think they would have made a footnote or something?"

I want to believe him. I want so badly to believe that my dad loved my mother—and me—that he helped us get away from Hoyt and the others. But the part of me that's been angry my whole life won't let me. The part that watched my mother and Aunt Charlotte die refuses to believe that my father is alive and well, somewhere, while my life has gone to hell in a hand basket.

He interrupts my dark musings. "There's one person who would know."

I stop pacing in front of him. "Hoyt. He would know whether his twin brother is alive and whether he betrayed the cause for my mother."

He stands and says, "Yeah, I'll bet he even knows your dad's location, where he's hiding out. He knew everything about *you*, didn't he?"

"You're right, but he's not going to just offer up that info."

"No, we'll have to take it from him." His stormy eyes are shadowed with emotion.

"You have a plan?" He's so close I can see the stubble on his face.

"Give me till morning. You'll have to take the information from his mind then escape, but I'm going with you when you leave. I need to find my mom and put her someplace safe if she's still alive."

"I can't see into his mind, Wyck. I've tried that. He's way too strong," I say, stepping back away from his striking face.

"You might, with this." From his back pocket he pulls out a small, metal ring attached to two leather straps.

"Give me your hand" He holds out his own. When he touches my fingers, I don't feel that same tingle that Easton's touch brings. In some way, that lack of feeling makes me feel better.

He slides my hand through one strap, which fits snuggly around my wrist. The ring, an odd, almost iridescent metal attached to the strap, fits dead center of my palm, exactly where my power emanates. At the top of the ring sits another, shorter strap made to loop around my middle finger, ensuring the ring stays put. It reminds me of releases archers use to pull back their bow strings.

"Is this—" I begin to ask, turning my hand over.

"Carter's device? Yep," he replies, still holding my hand in his.

"But how did you get it?"

He smiles deviously. "I'm a curious lad, Vivian, and Carter loves to hear himself talk. A few questions, a little boost to his enormous ego, and presto! He told me he how it works and that it was finished except for testing it."

"But how did you *get* it?" I ask again, trying to gently pull my hand away without offending him.

"I took it. I waited till he went on break, I broke in, and took it." He shrugs, holding tightly and either not noticing or pretending not to notice I'm trying to reclaim my hand.

"But won't he notice it's missing, Houdini?" I ask raising my brows.

"Never fear, princess. He had a lot of prototypes, so I took the one that looks the most like this one and switched them out."

"What kind of metal is this?" The coolness of it surprises me, almost like it's been refrigerated.

"I don't know, but from what he said, it's made of a similar material as the bonds they used on you when you arrived."

"But those things *hindered* my abilities."

"This will focus them, make them more precise." At my look of confusion, he sighs. "Because of the material, the ring will act like a seal. Your powers will be forced out of the ring, kind of like water through a narrow pipe. If it works correctly, the blasts should be amplified," he explains.

"You sound like Carter." I roll my eyes.

He grins again and leans in beside my ear, his stubble tickling my cheek. "Yeah, but I'm a whole lot sexier."

Shaking my head, I push him away playfully, and he stumbles back then falls on the bed, arms spread wide to match his grin. "Face it, princess. You know it's true."

Ignoring his remark, I ask, "But how will that help me get answers from Hoyt? You think blasting him, even with this thing"—I raise my hand—"will get him to talk? I threw a freakin' flaming van at him, and he survived. He's a lot stronger than you know."

He closes his eyes. "Use your head. If it amps your firepower, odds are it will increase that mind stealing shit you do." He rises up on his elbows. "When you put your hand on his head, you should be able to get any info you want, regardless of his mental might. It's a good thing you met me and I think you're hot, or you'd be stuck here forever!" He smiles teasingly.

"Really? Alright, would my hero like to test it out?" I sit down next to him and wiggle my fingers in his face.

"Are you challenging me?" he asks, pretending to be insulted.

"I believe I am. Of course, your brain's not exactly hard to read." I shrug superiorly.

He grabs my hand, jerking me down almost on top of him when he flops back. "Do your worst. But I warn you, I can't be held responsible for what you might see. There were several damsels who wouldn't take no for an answer before you came along, princess." With his devilish good looks, I have no doubt there were.

He positions my hand on the side of his face; my fingers brush against his petal-soft lashes and rest in his silky curls. His navy eyes darken to nearly black as his smile is replaced by a rare, thoughtful expression. When I close my eyes, sensations overwhelm me. The drumming of his heartbeat drowns out my own. Adrenaline rushes through me. I reign in some of my power, afraid of what might happen to us both if I don't.

Before I have time to adjust to the assault on my psyche, images and conversations bombard me—a barrage of faces and memories, like a movie in fast-forward. I see twin boys, shockingly similar as young children, helping a blond man build a tree house; boys opening Christmas presents in the arms of a beautiful, dark-haired woman with blue eyes; boys with baseball gloves arguing heatedly over a broken window. The same boys, older and more like their present selves, learning to drive with the blond man gripping the dashboard; awkward double dates; a winning shot in overtime of a basketball game; turkey dinners around a wide table; and finally a casket being lowered into the ground and the brunette crying uncontrollably in Wyck's arms.

Overwhelmed, tears scald my own cheeks until blackness drifts in. When the images stop and I open my eyes, Wyck stares back, clutching my hand against his chest. His eyes plunder my soul. I swipe embarrassingly at my tears, but he holds tightly and presses both of his hands over mine on his chest.

"Now you see why I have to get out of here?" he asks quietly.

I can only nod, my throat tight from keeping back the flood of emotions. He releases me and sits up, swooning slightly and grabbing his head.

"Are you okay?" I gasp, reaching for him.

"Yeah, I just…" He takes a steadying breath and drops his hands from his head. "It was intense. Felt like you were turning my head upside-down and shaking out my brain."

"Stronger than before?" I ask, hoping it will be enough to break down Hoyt's brain.

"Unquestionably." Then serious Wyck is gone, and Wyck the Wicked returns full force, trying to retrieve his cool factor. "See anything you wanna try?" He pats the bed and wiggles his brows.

"You're incorrigible, you know that?" I smile.

He lies back. "Ah, princess, you have no idea."

CHAPTER THIRTY-SIX

"ARE YOU READY?" Wyck, standing too close as usual, whispers behind me.

After the mind melting experiment, we came up with a plan—sort of. Our first task is to tell Easton, Cooper, and Abby about the plan, so they can be ready when the time comes to retrieve them.

"As I'll ever be," I reply, shoving the last of my belongings into my backpack. Wyck also has a pack strapped across his shoulders. "Did you tell Griffin yet?"

He shakes his head. "He didn't come back to our room last night. Before he left, he told me Matthews needed him for something. My guess is he went on a mission. I have to find him before we escape." His expression is serious, his jaw clenched.

"If he's out, I'll bet Hoyt is, too." I visualize the entire plan imploding.

"We'll just have to find out. I refuse to give up without even trying. Even if I can't talk to Griffin, I've got to leave and find Mom. I know getting info on your dad from Hoyt is important, but if he's gone, it might make this escape easier."

I know he's right, but I can't leave without finding out *something*. "If they aren't back in time, you'll take Easton, Cooper, and Abby, find where the river runs through the mountain, and escape in one of the boats I saw in Wallis's mental map of this place. I'll stay behind."

"No! No!" he exclaims shaking his head, pointing his finger at my chest. "You will not stay behind! You're going even if I have to drag you out! Besides the boy toy will never leave without you."

"He may have no choice. Besides, if he knows we've been together again, he might be happy to leave."

"What are you talking about? Something I should know?" he asks, brows drawn together in confusion.

"Let's go. I'll explain on the way." I step into the hall. "Did you take care of the surveillance?" Before he left last night, we decided Wyck would pay an early visit to Patricia and trick her into the storage closet—figured it was best *not* to know how—where he would lock her in somehow so that we could travel more freely around the compound.

"Didn't have to. Ferguson's on duty in there, and I saw Lilah walking toward the surveillance room. I have a feeling he'll be busy for a while." He wiggles his brows.

"Yuck, say no more." I make a gagging sound.

As we twist and turn toward the prisoners' quarters, I explain how Easton and I have a mental connection and how recently he's been able to see and hear me at times even when I'm not around.

"So, let me get this straight. Your boyfriend saw our dream kiss in your head?"

"Uh, *your* dream kiss, but yeah, that's about right."

"Great. We haven't even met, and he wants to kill me already," he says, sighing.

"Don't be so dramatic. I'm sure most people want to kill you immediately after meeting you, so this is not that different than what you're used to." I smile at my own joke.

"Very funny, princess. I'm only sayin' that if you were my girl-friend, and I even *thought* a guy wanted to kiss you, I'd be ready to rip his head off. And whether it's real or not, this kid saw us making out."

"No, he didn't! He saw you dreaming about us making out. There's a huge difference." Deep down, I'm incredibly flattered by what he just said, but I refuse to tell him that and inflate his Hindenburg-sized ego any more than it already is. "It's okay, Wyck. If you're afraid, I'll protect you. He's an athlete, you know. He has *huge* muscles." I can't resist teasing him if only to get a rise out of him—keeps my mind off the fact that we are all about to risk our lives.

"I'm not afraid of him," he says slowly, emphasizing each word. "But I'll fight him for you if that's what you want."

I turn, expecting to see him giving me that spicy grin, but he isn't looking at me, and he isn't smiling. Shit! This is going to get very

complicated. Continuing on in awkward silence, we eventually get
to the cell entrance where I pop open the door and rush inside.

At the sound of the door, Cooper sits up and rubs his eyes sleep-
ily. Then he jumps up from the cot beside Abby's and runs to the
bars. "Vivian! Please tell me we're gettin' outta here soon," he says,
holding onto the bars.

"Today, if everything goes right. I don't have much time in here,
Coop. Pack the backpacks, and be ready." I look around him at
Abby lying so still on the cot. Her eyes are closed. "How is she?"

"Better actually. She was awake for a while last night and ate a
little." He looks around, too. "But we need to get her outta here
fast. This place… it's like it's drainin' her. She doesn't wanna eat
or talk, and you know if she doesn't wanna talk, something's not
right." He's not smiling. Clearly, Abby's illness is taking its toll on
him. "I'm scared of what might happen if we don't leave pretty
damn quick."

"Will she be able to move today?" Wyck asks from beside me. I
had forgotten he was even there until just now.

Cooper, registering Wyck's presence for the first time, pulls back
to assess him. "Who the hell are you?"

I draw his attention back to me. The last thing we have time for
is a lot of questions. "His name is Wyck. He's been helping me, and
he's going with us. Will she be able to go?" I repeat Wyck's question.

Coop puffs out his chest. "Oh, she'll be ready. I'll carry her the
whole way if need be."

I lean in and kiss Cooper's cheek, which immediately turns red
with embarrassment. "Thank you, Coop, for taking such good care
of her. When we get out of here, you two can go someplace safe, and
you'll never have to see me again." I nearly tear up at the thought of
losing them for a second time, but Abby's parents' money can buy
them anonymity, and that's more important.

"Let's just focus on gettin' out for now," he says, smiling his
patented Cooper grin, promising the world is a good place, and
everything will be okay.

I move on toward Easton's cell. He's been standing at the bars,
listening to our conversation. As we approach, his eyes move over
my face and body as if he's making sure I'm okay. I haven't seen
him since before retrieving Zeb and my beach mission with Hoyt.

"Are you okay, Vivian?" His voice is strained, not like him at all.

"I'm fine. I came to—"

"Yeah, I heard." He motions with his chin toward Cooper's cell. "This is him, isn't it?" He glares at Wyck and grits his teeth.

"Easton, this is Wyck. Wyck, meet Easton." Neither smiles; in fact, neither of them moves a muscle, the tension thick, like waiting for a bomb to explode.

"We don't have time for a pissing contest, guys. Easton, be ready. We'll have to move fast, and you may have to help Coop with Abby." I kiss him quickly, squeeze his hand, and turn to go.

Wyck lingers a minute longer then begins to follow till Easton's voice stops us both. "Keep your hands off her, asshole. She's mine!" he yells.

Wyck smiles roguishly. "I wouldn't be so sure of that." Then he walks on past me while I stare open-mouthed at his back. "Come on, Vivian," he calls over his shoulder.

Throwing up both hands and shaking my head, I follow. When we have the door closed behind us, I turn on him. "What was that? Why did you say that?"

He shrugs. "Just amusing myself, princess. I'm about to risk my life for that dick. The least he could do is keep his mouth shut."

"Let's just find Hoyt and do this, okay?" I deliberately won't let myself think about what's going to happen when Easton is no longer behind bars. It won't be pretty.

As we head back to the main part of the facility, I try to focus on the job ahead of us. "Do you have any idea where we'll find Griffin?" I ask, knowing that Wyck wants to tell Griffin the truth about their father's death. I rub my fingers over the cool metal ring of Carter's device in my pocket.

"I thought we'd check the room first." He turns down our hallway. "If we're lucky, he'll be back." As soon as the words are out, we both notice the door to their room is slightly open. Wyck speeds up.

"Griffin, you in here?" he asks, pushing the door the rest of the way open.

Griffin's hair is dripping onto his bare shoulders. Dressed only in shorts and socks, he is yanking clothes from a chest drawer and tossing them onto the bed. He hardly spares us a glance as he continues to dress.

"Oh, hey, Wyck," he says, distractedly. "You been at breakfast?"

Wyck's eyes dart to the clock beside the bed where Griffin sits pulling on a fresh uniform. "It's only 5:30, Griff. They aren't even serving breakfast yet. Where've you been? And where're you going?"

"I can't tell you." He gives him an 'I'm sorry' face. "I have to leave as soon as I'm dressed, but I'm really glad you came in." This time he smiles and stands to pull up his uniform top. "Commander Matthews says when I finish this mission we might get to see Mom. I know you've been kinda worried."

Wyck cuts his eyes to me, then back to Griffin. "We need to talk. You better sit." He motions to the bed and puts his backpack on the floor.

"I'll wait outside," I say moving toward the door. But Wyck stops me.

"No, Vivian, please stay." Wyck begins pacing, his signature move when he's nervous. I sit down next to Griffin.

"What is it, Wyck? I'm kind of in a hurry." Griffin reaches for his boots.

"Your mission can wait. This is important."

"So is my mission." Griffin begins to stand, but Wyck pushes him back down. Griffin's eyes grow round, and he blinks repeatedly. I'll bet Wyck has never so much as yelled at Griffin in years.

"I wanted to break this to you gently, but you're not giving me much choice." He takes a deep breath. "Dad wasn't really killed in a terrorist attack." When Griffin doesn't stop him, Wyck hurries on before he loses his nerve. "The Liaisons killed him. They arranged an attack that would ensure Dad's death. Had Mom's car started that day, she'd be dead, too." He gestures around in disgust. "These people are using you, and we have to get out of here."

When he stops, Griffin doesn't speak; he doesn't yell or cry. He simply stares at Wyck. "Say something, Griffin!" Wyck exclaims.

"I know," Griffin says quietly.

"What?" Wyck asks, drawing back his head as though he's trying to see the solution to a puzzle and is standing too close.

"I know about Dad," Griffin replies just as calmly as before. "Commander Matthews told me two weeks ago."

Wyck's face blanches, and his breathing becomes rapid. "You know? Have known for weeks? And you're still working for them?"

"Commander Matthews explained that Dad would never have agreed to let us come here. They approached Dad about us right after I used my power accidentally that first time at the mall. Dad didn't want us to become everything we're supposed to become. He wanted us to be normal," he says the word as though it leaves a bad taste in his mouth then leaps up and grasps Wyck by the upper arms. "Commander Matthews didn't think you were ready to hear it yet, but don't you see! We're meant for greatness, Wyck!"

"And Mom? What about her?"

"Oh, Mom was never in any danger! He told me they deliberately messed up the car so she wouldn't be there!"

"And you believe that shit, Griffin? You really think Mom's not in danger? Think about it! We haven't spoken to her in forever!" Wyck's face has morphed from white to red; his fists are clenched at his sides.

"Of course, she's fine, and you will be, too, once you accept our fate."

"How did they do it? How did they brainwash you so completely?" Wyck shakes off Griffin's hands. "So that little scene with Lilah in the plane was for what? To keep me from figuring it out until Commander Matthews thinks it's time?"

"No, she was threatening you. I wasn't going to let her say those things to you. She has her purpose, but she's not really one of the Liaisons. Commander Matthews told me he keeps her out of missions as much as he can. He doesn't trust her." Griffin finishes with a shake of his head. From the expression in his eye, he seems to truly believe everything he's saying.

Wyck rubs his forehead and sighs. "Griffin, I'm leaving—today. Come with me please."

"I can't." He stands straighter. "I'm important here. I won't leave."

I stand and touch Wyck's shoulder. He looks down into my eyes, tears glisten in the indigo depths of his. He reaches for his bag and slings it onto his back. "We're going."

"I can't let you leave, Wyck. You only need a little more time then you'll manifest, and you'll understand why this is so important." He turns his gaze on me. "And, Vivian, I thought you would already see how important you are after your mission a few days ago."

"No, Griffin, if anything, I see why I *can't* stay. I'm going, too." Griffin has obviously stepped over into the land of the loony, and it's clear we're going to have a problem.

"I'm really sorry then." Griffin closes his eyes, and in the second it takes me to realize what he's doing, I'm already too late.

"No, Griffin, stop!" I grab his uniform front.

He opens his eyes, and we're nose to nose.

"What, what is it?" Wyck steps close to me.

"We're going to have company." I turn to Wyck. "Griffin just sent Hoyt a message." Looking back at Griffin, I ask, "Does he have his full power even with the equalizers on?"

When Griffin doesn't answer, Wyck pushes me aside and steps between us. "Answer her. Can Matthews use all of his powers?"

Griffin shakes his head. "No, not since the extra equalizer was installed. He can only use the mental power."

Wyck looks from me to Griffin. "We can't leave him free."

"I know." He pulls Griffin into a bone-crushing hug, holding on for several seconds before he whispers, "I'm sorry, brother." With the speed and force I remember from his workouts, he punches Griffin hard in the jaw, and Griffin falls backward onto the bed. Wyck, looking as though he might throw up, rubs his hand.

"Carry him to the bathroom. If we lock him inside, he'll be safe from… well, from whatever is about to happen." Wyck knows I don't want to hurt Griffin, and with Griffin's attitude about the Liaisons, I might be forced to unless we keep him locked up.

He hefts Griffin up around the midsection, and dragging his legs, Wyck manages to get him inside the small bathroom.

"Now what? It locks from the inside. I guess I could drag some furniture in front of the door," he says uncertainly.

"I've got a better idea." Slipping Carter's device from my pocket and onto my hand, I grasp the doorknob. Within a minute, it glows orange in my hand.

"Are you melting the knob?" Wyck asks, seemingly impressed. "Nice, but are you sure it will work?"

I chuckle softly. "Oh yeah, it'll work. Trust me."

I'm about to pull my hand away from the knob when the room door opens forcefully behind us. Hoyt's black eyes quickly take in the melted knob and the device. He knows that I can use my powers, but to his credit, instead of running back out, he slowly closes the door.

"Well done, my dear. You have found a way to defuse the power of my equalizer."

"Would you expect any less of me, *Uncle*?" Surprise flares in his face before he composes himself and gives a small bow of his head.

"Well done, again, Vivian. I won't bother asking how you know." Pausing, he moves his gaze to Wyck. "He's telling me everything I need to know. Planning an escape? My, my, how daring of you!" He laughs drily.

Wyck jerks his head to me, but I just sneer at Hoyt. "No, we aren't 'planning' an escape. We're *going* to escape, but before we go, you're going to tell me where to find my dad."

He continues to smile. "Really? And why would I do that? Your father, my"—he smirks—"brother, is a traitor. We could have been unstoppable! But he allowed your mother to get into his head and ruin our perfect plan."

Though his voice is still calm, his body radiates tension, his stance rigid. "You said 'is.' That means he's alive. I need to know where to find him." I step close and extend my hand toward his head, my palm already glowing blue inside the circle of the device.

"And you think this device of Carter's will actually allow you to hear my thoughts?" He motions to Wyck. "His brain is much less complex than mine. Oh, and I was deeply affected by your love for your mother, Wyck," he scoffs mockingly. "Very moving how she cried in your arms. I wonder how she's doing…" He trails off, curling his lip.

"You bastard!" Wyck lunges for Hoyt, but I step in front of him while Hoyt laughs again.

Without hesitating, I slap my hand to the side of his head. Those soulless eyes widen. "Yeah, I think it'll work just fine," I say as his thoughts begin to rush into me. But I've underestimated the force of our joining. Just like with Wyck, memories slam into me, but Wyck only had eighteen years of them, and he hasn't traveled the world committing atrocities against innocent people. My stomach churns at the sights of the dead and dying, people begging for mercy or fighting for their lives. Both our bodies tremble, and I struggle to stay upright and keep my eyes open. As if from a great distance, I notice the lights in the room are flickering, and I hear Wyck yelling, but I can't make out what he's saying.

Hoyt throws block after block, trying to break our connection.

Stop this before it's too late, Vivian! You don't have the control that you think you do! You'll kill us both!

Show me what I want to see, or I swear I won't stop until we're dead!

He's weakening. His eyes flutter then close. Images of identical blond boys with bright green eyes spin in my head, boys playing in this facility and the cave outside, boys running and yelling—not so different from Wyck's own memories. As the years rush by, the boys grow to men, and Hoyt's eyes begin to darken.

I feel a tugging at my hand. Wyck is trying to break our connection. I want to scream, tell him I'm so close, but I can't speak.

Hoyt's emotions begin to shift wildly—pride in his brother for taking on such an important mission, jealousy that he can no longer blend in enough to volunteer himself, humiliation at his brother's weakness, and then fear that he will be forced to destroy his own brother.

The next image is so clear, I know it must be their last minutes together, but Hoyt's weakness threatens to pull us both into oblivion. Mountains tower in the distance. Falling snow piles on tree limbs. I see their faces, the tears on both of their cheeks, but their voices are muffled and faint, like a movie with the sound turned down.

No! Don't you do this! Stay with me, Hoyt!

The image darkens then disappears. There is only a black void. My heavy eyes close. My knees buckle.

"Vivian! Vivian, wake up!" His voice is frantic, panicked. "So help me, princess, I'll strip you down and throw your ass into a cold shower if you don't open your eyes right now!"

"Not if you want to live," I mumble, forcing my sluggish brain into action.

Before I've even gotten my eyes completely open, Wyck is holding me against him. "Thank God! I thought you were dying!"

"I might still if you don't let me breathe," I squeak out. He loosens his hold, and I swoon, sinking back against the mattress.

"Easy, princess." He runs to his bag and pulls out a bottle of water. His hands shake so badly that he can barely open it. "Here, small sips."

But I yank it from his hands, slosh a good deal on the bed, and chug it down. My entire body feels like it's burning from the inside out. I almost expect to see smoke coming from my ears. My brain feels like mush, and my limbs are weak as if I've been running for miles. Hoyt's body lies motionless on the floor where he was standing before our mind melding.

"Is he dead?" I ask, not completely sure how the thought of his death makes me feel. He felt betrayed by my dad; I feel betrayed by both of them, but he's still my only connection to my father. I didn't get to see everything I wanted to see. I need him alive—for now.

Wyck checks his pulse. "No, he has a pulse. It's weak, but he's still alive. I hope you got what you needed because I'm not sure you'll get anything from him for a while, maybe never. That was pretty powerful. You might have destroyed his mind."

"I didn't get it all. I need to go back into his head." I ignore his comment about destroying Hoyt's mind. I refuse to think about it.

"Vivian, look at him! Now is the perfect time to escape. He's not coming around, and the only other person who can stop us is locked in the bathroom. Let's go while we have a chance!"

He grabs both our bags and opens wide the door to a surprised Lewis who has his hand raised as if to knock. Lewis looks from Wyck to me to Hoyt on the floor and pulls his gun before either Wyck or I can react.

"Lewis, no!" I scream and think to jump up from the bed, but my exhausted body isn't moving.

He fires the gun.

"Stop!" Wyck yells.

I brace for the impact and squeeze my eyes closed, seeing Easton's face and wishing I could tell him I love him one last time. But when I don't feel the bullet slam into me, I peek with one eye then I open both eyes wide. There, six inches from my chest, is the bullet, frozen like a slow-motion movie moment. Lewis still stands at the open door with the gun raised and his expression fierce, but like the bullet, he isn't moving.

Wyck rushes from the door to me and pulls me left, out of the bullet's path.

I can only stare. "You did it, Wyck! You stopped time!" I wrap my arms around him and squeeze with all my might. "You manifested!"

But, always the strategist, he pushes me back. "Yeah, I guess I did. Now move! We don't know how long it will last!"

He pulls me toward the door, and we shove past Lewis's still form. But when we're in the hall, he hauls me against him and kisses me hard and fast on the lips.

Winking, he says, "You can thank me later."

CHAPTER THIRTY-SEVEN

RUNNING BREATHLESSLY, we reach the prisoners' quarters, force open the door, and sprint down the hallway to Cooper and Abby. Cooper already has two packs on his shoulders and is wrapping Abby in a blanket. She's awake, and her face lights up when she sees us.

"Vivian! Are we really getting out?" she asks. The paleness of her face and the dark circles under her eyes attest to her illness, but her eyes are bright, and she sounds like the old Abby.

"Yes, Ab, we are." I smile as I place my hand on the locking panel and the door opens easily. "Wyck, start moving them to the tunnel leading downriver. I'll get Easton and be right behind you."

Without waiting, I run to Easton's cell. He too is packed and ready. As soon as I open his cell, he grabs my hand, and we run down the hallway not far behind the others.

We cut across the cave and into the natural tunnel leading to the river. The sound of water covers our steps, and a cool mist dampens my face. I hope Wallis's memory is accurate, and the boats are still docked close by.

At the end of the tunnel, the cave opens wide again, and sure enough, a boat dock with three large boats sits right in front of us. Wyck is holding Abby while Cooper jumps inside one of the boats, readying a place for her. He pulls up the top of one of the wide seats lining the side and drags out a life jacket which he throws on top of the seat before reaching out to take Abby back into his arms.

As he sits her on the seat and begins to fasten the jacket around her, I can see her frown, and her mouth moves in what I assume is complaint, probably about the olive green color. I can't keep from smiling because I know she's going to be her old self in no time.

Wyck positions himself behind the boat's steering wheel and turns the key, starting the engine. I motion for Easton to get in. He shakes his head.

You first. I'll untie the boat then jump in.

No, I want to put holes in the other boats, so they can't follow. Get in. I'll be right behind you.

He stands uncertainly for a second then climbs inside, taking Cooper and Abby's bags as he does.

Moving to the first stall, I raise my hand and send a blast large enough to put a hole about twelve inches wide in the side. Water begins to bubble in, but just to be on the safe side, I focus on how scared I am right now, and the water rushes in, quickly overtaking the boat. As I move to the second boat, movement from the tunnel entrance catches my eye. Ferguson is running down the tunnel toward us.

I lock eyes with Wyck.

Take them and go, Wyck! Ferguson will kill us all!

No, I won't leave you behind! I'll just stop time, and you can jump in—

You've only done it once. We don't have time to see if it will work. Just go, please, Wyck. Don't let me down. I'll follow. I promise.

Easton is looking from me to Wyck as if he knows what's about to happen. Bracing his hands on the side, he begins to vault from his seat, but Wyck throws the boat in reverse and quickly pulls away from the dock, slamming Easton down into his seat again.

I love you, Easton. I will find you.

CHAPTER THIRTY-EIGHT

I BLAST THE SECOND BOAT. No matter how this thing goes, I don't want him following the others. No sooner have I finished with the second boat, Ferguson, gun drawn, emerges from the tunnel. I raise my hand, but as I'm about to fire, he's jerked off his feet and backward into the tunnel. His gun flies into the air then skids across the rock floor into the hungry river. I race toward the tunnel just as Wallis yanks Ferguson to his feet and punches him forcefully in the jaw.

As Ferguson slides unconscious down the glistening rock, Wallis turns to me. Straining to be heard over the water's roar, he yells, "Vivian, what are you doing?"

"I have to go, Wallis! I'm sorry, but I won't let you stop me!" His eyes search mine. I really don't want to hurt him, and I'm about to brainjack him when he lifts his wrist and yells into his radio.

"Send a medic! No sign of the prisoners!" To me he shouts, "Go, I'll stall as long as possible!"

"But, Wallis, what will they do to you when they find out?"

"I'll tell them you forced me! Don't worry about me, Vivian. Just go!"

Pulling him in for a quick hug, I say near his ear, "Thank you, Wallis." And I run to the water's edge. Glancing back at Wallis with his hand raised in farewell, I see Ferguson step out of the tunnel, his Taser aimed at Wallis's back.

"Look out!" I scream, but Wallis goes down, his body jerking grotesquely. Ferguson removes his eye patch, and the cave begins to shake.

The shaking knocks us both down as stalactites break from the cave ceiling high above, crashing violently into the river and the dock. Water splashes me and the already slick rock bank. The cave groans angrily.

Ferguson crawls on his hands and knees back to the tunnel, covering his eye once again, but even after he's in the safety of the tunnel, the cave continues to rumble. When a fissure several feet wide spreads across the ceiling, huge chunks of rock smash around me.

Fifteen feet away, Wallis still lies unconscious while rock rains around him. I create an energy shield, but it isn't big enough to reach him. I try to stand, but the force of the quake forces me back down. As I belly crawl toward him, a massive slab of stone breaks from the ceiling and slams into Wallis, landing on his back.

"NO!" I scream, rushing toward him, but the stones continue to fall between us. When I'm a foot or two away, I know I'm too late. Nothing I do will help Wallis now. If I don't go soon myself, his sacrifice will have been for nothing.

I stumble and slide back to the riverbank; rocks bounce from my energy shield, but my earlier episode with Hoyt has depleted my energy, and the shield begins to waver. Before my energy is completely gone, I have one last task.

Turning to the tunnel, I raise my hand and fire with every ounce of my remaining strength. Not even when I battled Hoyt in the park did I fire this forcefully, and the already weakened cave wall crumbles. Rock fills the tunnel opening and continues to fall as I leap into the river and will it to carry me to Easton.

*   *   *

I awake in Easton's arms, sputtering and coughing. I don't remember the trip downriver nor do I remember being pulled into the boat. My arms and legs feel like lead, and every part of me hurts.

He sighs and holds me tightly to his chest. "You have to stop doing that, babe. You're gonna give me gray hair." He smiles teasingly down at me, but I barely have the energy to smile back. His face turns serious. "Are you okay? What do you need me to do?"

"Only this," I whisper, feeling his familiar strength seep into me little by little.

"So what happens now? What do we do?" Wyck's voice from behind the steering wheel jars me.

"Leave her alone. Can't you see she just about killed herself to save us?" Easton snaps.

"The way I see it, I saved *you*! I only wanted to know where to go from here." Wyck snarls as he shifts the boat into gear again and speeds us farther from the facility.

"You're not going anywhere with us!" Easton yells.

"Stop," I say, but the noise from the engine covers my voice.

"Wanna bet? I'll go anywhere I damn well please, and you can't stop me!"

"Listen, you two," Cooper pipes up, but they ignore him.

"Wyck, Easton," I mumble into Easton's chest.

"You are not coming with us!" Easton jabs his finger in Wyck's direction, and I nearly topple to the floor.

"Guys," I say louder, stronger with the force of Easton's emotions surging through me.

"YOU DON'T EVEN KNOW WHERE WE'RE GOING!" Wyck screams back.

"NEITHER DO YOU!" Easton yells.

I wrench away from him and sit up. "Stop it, both of you! *I* know where we're going!"

EPILOGUE

"VIRGINIA, LOOK AT ME!" Ethan yelled. "Do not think of him now! Think only of the babe!"

His blue-green gaze pleaded with hers, but she wanted only to let the pain take her, to drown in her tears. "But how will I raise the child alone, Ethan?" she asked, grasping the metal sides of the table.

"You'll *not* be alone. I will be father to your child. He will be ours. I love you, Virginia." Steadying himself against the table, he leaned close, brushed the hair from her feverish face, and tenderly kissed her lips with all the love he felt for her and the child she carried. Though the babe would never be his by blood, he knew he would yield every drop of his to keep the babe safe.

"I will take care of you both," Ethan promised, and Virginia felt his assurance in the strength of the hand that now held hers.

Suddenly, burning pain tore through her. She sat up, pushing against it and grabbing the pole attached to the corner.

"Virginia, you must push now!" Lord St. Clair shouted as thunder boomed directly above them. A jagged streak of lightning shot from the clouds and hit one of the metal rods where it stretched through the building's roof and into the dark sky. Nature's strongest force sped down the length of metal and straight into Virginia's right hand.

For a moment, time held its breath while the force of the strike traveled through Virginia, the babe, and Ethan where he gripped her hand and the table. A brilliant blue light filled the room.

Lord St. Clair shielded his eyes from his position on the floor where the blast had thrown him. He expected to find them all three dead when the glowing stopped, but when he uncovered his eyes, not only were all three alive, but Virginia's strength seemed renewed, her still-glowing hand where she gripped the pole the only evidence of the lightning.

"Ethan?" she asked in confusion as if he could explain what had happened.

"I am well, Virginia. Is the babe...," he trailed off, unwilling to ask if the child he had grown to think of as his own had perished.

"She is ready to meet her father," she replied with a shy smile.

" 'She?'" His brows drew together. "'Tis a girl? But how do you know?"

"She told me." Virginia gripped the pole and Ethan's hand and pushed with all of her renewed strength. Lord St. Clair jumped to his feet, and when the babe took her first breath, he handed her to Virginia.

Ethan grabbed a piece of the spare linen and helped Virginia wrap the child whose cry filled the room and made them both smile. Virginia held her close and spoke softly until the cries ceased.

"What shall we name her, Ethan?" Virginia asked, gazing into his peaceful eyes and knowing he was her destiny.

He gazed thoughtfully at her tiny face. "We'll call her Vega after one of the brightest stars in the heavens." He touched her cheek, and she turned her tiny face toward his hand.

ACKNOWLEDGMENTS

Thank you Olivia and Wyatt for understanding that sometimes mommy needs to work and to Chris for actually reading my first book! Thank you (again) to Katie and Kim for all your advice and support. I love you all!

Thank you to all of my readers. I couldn't do this without you!

Thank you to my Booktrope team, Samantha March, Cathy Shaw, Greg Simanson, and Jesse James Freeman. You guys are the best!

ABOUT THE AUTHOR

Andrea Murray has been teaching English for longer than most of her students have been alive. She lives in a very small town in Arkansas with her precocious daughter, energetic son, and NASCAR-loving husband. *Vicious* is the sequel to her first novel, *Vivid*. She has also written *Vengeance*, the third novel in the *Vivid Trilogy* and *Omni*, her newest young adult novel.

www.ingramcontent.com/pod-product-compliance
Lightning Source LLC
Chambersburg PA
CBHW020606250626
47154CB00004B/1388